Poltergeists
of
Petoskey

**Look for more 'American Chillers'
from AudioCraft Publishing, Inc.,
coming soon! And don't forget to pick
up these books in Johnathan Rand's
thrilling *'Michigan Chillers'* series:**

#1: Mayhem on Mackinac Island
#2: Terror Stalks Traverse City
#3: Poltergeists of Petoskey
#4: Aliens Attack Alpena
#5: Gargoyles of Gaylord
#6: Strange Spirits of St. Ignace
#7: Kreepy Klowns of Kalamazoo
#8: Dinosaurs Destroy Detroit
#9: Sinister Spiders of Saginaw
#10: Mackinaw City Mummies

American Chillers:
#1: The Michigan Mega-Monsters
#2: Ogres of Ohio
#3: Florida Fog Phantoms
#4: New York Ninjas
#5: Terrible Tractors of Texas
#6: Invisible Iguanas of Illinois
#7: Wisconsin Werewolves
#8: Minnesota Mall Mannequins
#9: Iron Insects Invade Indiana

and more coming soon!

AudioCraft Publishing, Inc.
PO Box 281
Topinabee Island, MI 49791

#3: Poltergeists
of
Petoskey

JOHNATHAN
RAND

An AudioCraft Publishing, Inc. book

Graphics layout/design consultant: Chuck Beard, Straits Area Printing

ISBN 1-893699-08-0

Printed in USA

Fifth Printing, June 2003

Poltergeists of Petoskey

Visit the official Michigan & American
Chillers web site at:

www.americanchillers.com

Featuring excerpts from upcoming stories, interviews, and
much MORE!

"Would you quit trying to scare me? Just go to sleep, will you?"

It was my twin brother, Adrian.

Here it was, the middle of the night, and he was standing at the door of my bedroom, scolding me for doing something — even though I was half asleep!

"What are you talking about?" I asked groggily. I was angry. It was late, and I didn't appreciate being awakened at such an hour. Even if it was summer, and even if I *did* get to sleep in a little.

"You," he hissed. He was mad! "Quit walking by my door and making noises!"

Huh? What was he talking about?

"I'm not walking by your door," I said,

yawning.

What would make him think such a thing? I had been sleeping. I'm not going to wake up in the middle of the night just to try and scare him!

"I heard you walk by my door," he continued, wagging a pointed finger in my direction. *"Again.* Just like last night."

It was hard to see him in the dark. He was just a dark shape that was standing in my doorway.

"You're crazy," I said. "I've been *sleeping!"*

"Yeah, well knock it off or I'm going to tell Mom and Dad."

Fine. Let him tell Mom and Dad. I was telling him the truth . . . I've been sleeping. Besides . . . why would I waste my time trying to scare Adrian in the middle of the night? It's easy enough to scare him during the day.

My name is Alexis, but everyone calls me Alex. I'm twelve. My brother Adrian and I are twins. Not identical twins, but fraternal twins. He's a boy, I'm a girl. And, if I do say so myself,

I was given a few more brains than my brother. Of course, he disagrees with me, but that just shows how wrong he can be.

I have lived in Petoskey my whole life. It's great here! I mean, since I haven't lived anywhere else, I guess I can't really say if there's anyplace better, but I sure do like Petoskey. It's a small city in northwest lower Michigan, right next to Lake Michigan. It's beautiful! There are lots of pretty beaches and forests and all kinds of things to do.

My favorite thing to do in the whole world is swim. I love swimming! I swim in pools, in the lake—anyplace where there is water! Adrian doesn't like the water as much as I do, but he likes going to the beach. We don't live very far from the Petoskey State Park, so he and I walk there a lot.

Last year, Mom and Dad started looking for a new house. They said that the one we lived in had become too small, and that we all needed more space. They said that I would get a bigger bedroom!

THAT would be great! I mean . . . I liked

the house that we were living in at the time . . . but Mom and Dad were right — it *was* kind of small.

Anyway, when Mom and Dad said that they had found a new house for us, I was really excited — until I saw it.

It was an *old* house!

An old farmhouse, to be exact. It sat in the middle of a field, cold and alone, and it looked like it had been empty for years! When Mom and Dad asked what we thought about it, I told them that I thought it was falling apart. It was true! Shingles had fallen off the roof, and there were holes through the walls. Who on earth could live in a house like that? It was a wreck — and Mom and Dad agreed!

But they said that if it was fixed up right, it would be beautiful once again. I didn't see how then, but *now* I do!

Mom and Dad bought the house and we spent last summer working on it. There was a lot of work that we had to do. Adrian and I helped with some of it. Mostly, we just hauled all of the old junk out to the big dumpster.

But Mom and Dad were right! After we fixed it up, it sure was beautiful. All of the rooms have hardwood floors and high ceilings. And lots and lots of room! Mom and Dad said that they wanted to make the house look just like it did when it was first built—way back in 1897!

Wow! We were going to live in a house that was over one hundred years old!

There was only one problem, and it was a big one: GHOSTS!

2

Now . . . before you think that I'm really weird or something, let me tell you . . . I had never believed in ghosts before . . . but I sure do now!

Here's what happened:

One night not long after we moved in, I was sleeping in my bedroom. Mom and Dad said I could decorate it any way that I wanted. My bedroom is really neat . . . I have paintings and pictures of horses on the walls. I even have a poster of a horse on my ceiling! I really like horses.

Anyway, I went to bed early, before anyone else. I was tired! I had been swimming most of the day, and then my friend Stacey and I went horseback riding. Stacey lives a couple miles away. They have a farm and a few horses. Dad says that we might get horses some day. I hope so.

I was tired when I got home, so I went to bed early. It was so early that the sun was still up.

The problem was, when I woke up, it was *dark*. I couldn't get back to sleep. The clock next to my bed said that it was almost four in the morning—but I was wide awake!

And I was thirsty. So I got up to get a glass of water.

Living in an old home is cool. But it can be spooky sometimes, too. When you walk on the old wood floor, it creaks and moans. Sometimes the house makes noises in the night. It was a bit scary the first couple nights, but I got used to it.

As I walked down the stairs, the steps creaked beneath my feet. Nothing unusual.

But when I got to the bottom of the stairs, the creaking sound continued!

I just stood there, looking up at the darkened staircase. I could hear the steps squeak, just like someone was walking on them . . . but there was no one there! I was terrified, but I was too afraid to even move.

Suddenly the squeaking stopped. The house got really quiet. Still, I was too afraid to move. I don't know how long I stood there in my nightgown, frozen to the floor, watching. Shadows loomed out at me like dark animals, waiting to attack.

After some time, I got up the courage to walk to the kitchen. In our kitchen we have a small stove light that stays on all the time. It gives off enough light to see pretty good in the dark.

I got a glass of water and gulped it down. When I sat it back on the counter, I noticed something strange.

All of the cupboard doors in the kitchen had opened! Not just a little bit, but all the way open! I knew that they were closed when I first walked into the kitchen.

So . . . I closed all of them. There were twelve cupboard doors that had opened. I stood there for a moment, looking at them, wondering if they would open up again.

They didn't.

Whew. That was too freaky.

I just left the kitchen and went back to bed. I was a little nervous going back up the stairs, thinking that I might hear the strange creaking on the steps again. I didn't, and I was glad. I crawled back into bed and finally was able to fall asleep.

When I awoke in the morning, the sun was already up. Birds were singing in the yard, and I heard an airplane buzzing high in the sky. I threw on my sweats and an old T-shirt, and went downstairs. Mom was in the kitchen.

"Hi Sweets," she said, kissing me on the cheek as I sat down on a stool. Mom has called me 'Sweets' for as long as I can remember.

"Good morning," I yawned. "Is there any juice left?"

Mom reached into the fridge and pulled out a pitcher. There was just enough orange juice left to fill a glass.

"Finish that up and I'll make some more. Your father and your brother will be up soon, and they'll want some."

She poured a glass and I sipped it. It was cold and sweet and tangy.

"Oh," she said, opening the freezer. She pulled out a can of frozen orange juice and ran it under hot water in the sink. "Did you get up and come downstairs last night?" she asked.

"Mm-hmm," I muttered, sipping on the glass of orange juice and nodding my head.

"I thought so. What on earth were you looking for?"

"What do you mean?" I asked, putting the empty glass down on the counter.

"The cupboard doors, of course. *All of them were open when I got up this morning.*"

3

Later that day, I told my brother about the cupboards.

"That's really weird," he said.

I couldn't figure out how those cupboard doors opened. It was like they opened all by themselves! I thought that maybe I just *dreamed* that I closed them when I got up to get a glass of water. At least, that's what I tried to tell myself.

But I wasn't really scared. I was sure that there had to be some reason. What that reason was, I didn't know.

Nothing happened the next night or the night after that. Actually, a few nights went by before something else happened. Something that scared the daylights out of me!

I had almost forgotten about the cupboard incident. Late one night I got up again to get a glass of water. I was sleepy and the house was dark. No one else was awake.

But when I got to the kitchen, there was already a glass of water poured! It even had ice in it. It sat right on the counter in plain view.

Freaky!

I didn't know if I should drink it or not. But no one else was awake. How a glass of ice water was poured in the middle of the night was a mystery.

So I drank it. It was icy-cold and good. I kept expecting Mom or Dad or Adrian to come into the room and ask me why I drank their water, but they never did.

After I finished it, I poured the ice into the sink, then set the glass onto the counter. It was still very late (or early, depending on how you looked at it) and I wanted to hop back into my warm bed.

I reached for the glass to place it in the dishwasher. Mom's real strict about that. If we use a dish or a glass, rinse it off and put it in the dishwasher, pronto. I reached for the glass.

It was full!

The glass sat on the counter, *filled with water and ice!*

Had I done it and forgot about it?

No, I hadn't. I was sure.

I looked in the sink. The ice was still there from when I had emptied the glass.

That freaked me out. I didn't even stay long enough to empty the glass and put it in the dishwasher. I'd explain to Mom in the morning. Right now I just wanted to curl up in bed and pull the sheets over my head!

I left the kitchen and tip-toed up the stairs. The steps cried out and protested beneath my bare feet. Then I remembered the other night, when the steps had continued to creak, even when there was no one there. When I reached the top of the stairs I stopped, expecting the stairs to keep squeaking. They didn't, and I was glad.

My bedroom door was open, and bright moonlight lit up the floor. My window was open and the night air was warm and fresh. I could hear thousands of crickets chiming in the field. It was the only sound I heard, and I had grown attached to the gentle whirring of the insects. The sound of crickets meant that it was time for sleep.

I felt better, I guess, hearing the crickets, and my fear left me. There had to be some explanation about the glass, I told myself. There *had* to be. Maybe Mom or Dad had left the glass out before they went to bed. Maybe they even left it for me. I would ask them in the morning. That didn't explain how the glass got re-filled, but there had to be some logical reason for that, too.

There *had* to be.

I stood for a moment looking out the open window. The field was glowing in the moonlight. It was beautiful.

When I turned to crawl back into bed, I caught my reflection in the mirror, and what I saw made me cold with fright.

There was someone else in the mirror! I could see the dark reflection of someone—or something—standing behind me!

4

"Ohhh!" I screamed.

Actually, I didn't really scream. I think I was too afraid! It sounded more like a loud drawing in of breath. Both of my hands flew up, covering my open mouth.

I spun.

It was Adrian!

I should have known! He was standing in my doorway in his pajamas.

"Geez," he snickered. "You sure get spooked easy!"

"That was *not* funny!" I scolded. And it wasn't.

"I wasn't trying to scare you," he said. "I heard a noise and I got up to see what it was. It as just you."

"I got up to get a glass of water," I explained coldly. "Is that illegal in my own home?" I was still shaking from the scare, and I was angry.

Then he did something that I couldn't believe! He apologized! Adrian *actually* apologized!

"Gosh, I'm sorry about that, Al," he said. "I really didn't mean to."

"That's okay," I said. "It's just that . . . well, there's a couple weird things that have been going on."

"Like the glass of water?" he asked.

He knew!

"How did you—was that *you?* Did you put the glass of water there?"

He shook his head from side to side. "Not me, Alex," he said. "But I've seen it a couple times. I go to get a glass of water, and it's already waiting. Then, after I drink it—"

" —it fills itself back up again," I said. He nodded in agreement. "And I suppose you've seen the cupboards too, huh?"

"Yes," I whispered. "They open and close by themselves."

Adrian shifted in the doorway.

"Gosh Al," he said quietly. "Do you think the house is . . . *haunted?* Do you think we live in a haunted house?"

"No way," I said. "There's no such thing as ghosts."

"But how do we explain the water glass filling up all by itself? And the cupboards opening by themselves? Something really weird is going on in this house, Alex. *Really* weird."

A chill snaked along my spine like a tiny mouse scurrying up and down my back. It was the way Adrian had said those two words:

Really weird.

He was right. There was something really weird going on, that was for sure.

But what?

"Remember a few nights ago?" he asked me. "Remember when I came to your bedroom and told you to stop trying to scare me?"

I nodded.

"Well, I heard something that night. Like

footsteps. Up and down the stairs and across the hall. It was just like someone was walking on the floor, only no one was there. That's why I thought you did it."

"It wasn't me," I whispered.

"I know that now . . . because now I hear the footsteps almost every night."

I shuddered. "I've heard them too," I said. "A couple of nights ago when I went down to the kitchen. When I got to the bottom of the stairs, the steps kept squeaking like there was someone walking on them."

We were silent for a moment, listening to the chorus of crickets drifting through the open window. The drapes fluttered softly in the gentle breeze, and the field was aglow by the light of the moon.

"What do we do?" I asked.

"Beats me," Adrian replied. "But it sure is freaking me out. I wish it would stop."

"Maybe if we asked it to go away, it would," I offered.

"*What* would?" Adrian wondered aloud. "We don't even know what—or who—this is.

We don't—"

"*Sssshhh!*" I whispered, placing a finger to my lips. *"I just heard something!"*

He stopped talking, and we listened.

Nothing. Just crickets.

Listening . . . .

"What did you hear?" Adrian whispered, leaning toward me so he wouldn't have to raise his voice any higher than he needed. "I don't—"

But he stopped short of his sentence.

Creeeaaakkkkk . . . kkkk . . . eeaakkkkk.

Adrian's eyes grew to the size of golf balls! I guess mine probably did, too.

Creaak . . . Creeeeeeeeee . . . eeeeek . . . .

It was louder. Whatever it was, it was coming closer. It was coming up the steps!

5

Creeeeee . . . eaaaaa . . . aaaccc . . . cckkkkkkk.

Adrian and I stood motionless, too afraid to move a muscle. The creaking continued. Whatever it was, it kept coming closer.

Then we could see a shadow! A dark shadow moving up the steps.

What could we do? Where could we go? There was no place to run . . . and I certainly wasn't jumping out the window!

The shadow fell over the top of the stairs — and then:

A voice!

"I thought I heard noises up here," it said.

Whew! It was only Dad!

"Man, you really scared us!" Adrian said.

I could hear the relief in his voice.

"I heard you talking downstairs," Dad said. "It's late. Go back to bed."

With that said, Dad turned and walked back downstairs. His shadow faded, and he was gone.

"Wow," Adrian said, breathing a sigh of relief. "I'm glad that it was just Dad."

"I'm going back to sleep," I said, and I crawled beneath the covers.

"See ya tomorrow," Adrian said. He turned, and I could hear the floor squeak as he walked back to his bedroom.

But I couldn't sleep. I just kept thinking about the creaking steps and the cupboard doors and the water glass. It really freaked me out!

I wondered about the people who had lived in the house before we did. Mom and Dad said that the old home hadn't been lived in for a long time.

Why?

Maybe ghosts chased everyone away, I thought. *Maybe someone knew that the house was haunted, so they left. They left and they never came back.*

I thought about those things for a long time. The crickets kept me company, and every once in a while I heard the hoot of an owl somewhere in the forest. I tried to think about animals, about crickets, about the warm air swishing in through my open window . . . but it didn't work. No matter how hard I tried, I kept thinking and wondering.

Could the house be haunted?

Could there actually be ghosts here? And if so, what would we do?

A million questions spun through my head, and I didn't have an answer to any of them.

I looked at the clock. It was almost four thirty in the morning.

But I couldn't go to sleep, no matter how hard I tried!

I pulled my covers up over my head, hoping maybe that would help.

Nope.

I counted sheep. I have heard that if you count sheep, it will help you fall asleep faster.

After I got to five hundred, I gave up. I figured that there was no way that I would get back to sleep. The only thing I could do was lay there in bed, waiting. Waiting for the sun to come up.

Suddenly, I heard a strange voice. It was very faint and quiet, but I was certain that it was a voice.

I sat up in bed, listening.

"Alexis . . . ."

It was my name! Someone was calling me!

There was no doubt about it. It was a voice, calling my name. It was coming from outside!

"Alexxxiiiiiiissssss . . . ."

Nobody calls me 'Alexis'. Only Mom or Dad. In fact, not many people even know that 'Alexis' is my full name.

But this voice was soft! It . . . it sounded like a girl . . . maybe about my age!

I was hunched up in bed, my arms wrapped around my knees, listening . . . .

"Alexis . . . I'm here . . . I'm outside . . . ."

If I thought I had been freaked out by the water glass and the open cupboard doors, it was *nothing* compared to what I was feeling now!

But who was it? I didn't recognize the voice.

There was only one way to find out.

I took a deep breath, slowly drew back the covers, stepped off the bed, and walked to the window.

6

What I saw just about scared the life right out of me.

It was still very dark, and the sky above was sprinkled with stars. The moon was high in the sky, but it was only a partial moon, like a big, bright thumbnail.

But there was something glowing in the field! It was a strange, misty-blue color, and it stayed in one place, shimmering in the darkness.

I was terrified. I rubbed my eyes.

This isn't real, I thought. *I'm going to open my eyes and whatever it is will be gone. It WILL be gone.* I held my hands over my eyes and counted the numbers in my head.

One . . . Two . . . Three . . . .

I opened my eyes.

Oh no!

It was closer! The strange blue object was now just below me in the yard!

But perhaps the strangest of all is that the 'object' wasn't an 'object' at all . . . it was a *girl!* I was *right!* I could make out her features quite well from where I was standing at the window. She was wearing a long dress, and her hair was in two braids. I wasn't sure what color her dress or her hair was, because the blue glow around her was so bright.

"Alexis," she called out quietly.

My terror turned to complete horror. I opened my mouth to scream but no sound came out. I tried to shout for Adrian, for Mom and Dad, for anyone . . . but I was too afraid.

"Alexxxxxxiiiiissssssss," her soft voice whispered.

I could only stare in disbelief as the form drifted closer still.

And her hand!

She kept motioning me to come toward her, like she wanted me to come outside!

Fat chance of that! I wasn't going

anywhere!

It was then that I noticed that the night had become very quiet and still. The crickets were no longer chirping, and there were no other sounds. Everything was strangely silent.

Finally, I couldn't take it any longer. I turned and dove headfirst into bed, pulled the sheets over my head, and curled up into a ball.

It has to be a nightmare, I told myself. *It was just a nightmare. A dream. Or my imagination. That's all it was.*

I was shaking in bed, and my teeth were chattering, but I listened for the voice.

Nothing.

Minutes passed. Still nothing. I grew more comfortable.

Yes, I thought. *That was all it was. A dream. A strange one at that, but it was only a dream.*

Slowly, I drew my hand up and pulled back the covers a tiny bit. I peered out with just one eye.

Nothing.

Or, at least, nothing that shouldn't be there. I could make out the shadows of my dresser and my desk. The window was open, and once again I heard the soothing chirps of crickets coming from the field.

I relaxed, letting out a sigh of relief.

A dream, I thought thankfully. *It was just a dream.*

But was it? I mean . . . it seemed so real. I could still see the glowing blue girl in my head, just like I had actually seen her.

Had I?

I had to know. If it was only a dream, then there was no reason to worry.

I pulled the covers down a bit more and swung my legs over the edge of the bed. The wood floor was cold beneath my feet.

I stood up quietly and slowly walked to the window.

Bright stars still twinkled in the dark sky. The crickets were singing, and there was no sign of any glowing blue figure. The girl I had seen was only in my head.

Suddenly there was a loud scream! It was so loud it made me jump.

But the scream wasn't coming from

outside . . . it was *inside!* It came from inside our house! I could hear it echoing through the halls and rooms.

And I recognized the voice! The wail bellowed out again.

It was Adrian!

7

Adrian's voice pierced the night.

"*Get away! Get away from me!*" he screamed.

Lights clicked on downstairs, and I heard the sound of thundering footsteps. I ran out into the hall just in time to see Mom and Dad bounding up the stairs. From his bedroom, Adrian was still screaming.

Now that Mom and Dad were there, I was brave enough to go find out what was going on. I ran to Adrian's room.

Mom was sitting on the bed, and Dad was standing. Adrian was hunched up, his covers drawn up over his knees and his chest.

"A ghost!" he exclaimed. His eyes were

wide and he was shaking. "It was a g-g-ghost! Right here in my room!"

"No, honey," Mom said. "There's no such thing as ghosts. It was only a dream."

"I'm t-t-t-telling you, I s-s-saw a g-g-g-ghost."

He was really scared!

And so was I. But I didn't say anything, and Adrian continued.

"I did! Really! Standing right there!" He pointed toward the center of his room. "She was wearing a dress! And she was kind of a fuzzy blue. It was like I could see right through her!"

Oh my gosh! Adrian had seen her, too!

"It was just a nightmare," Dad said. "Go back to sleep" He turned to leave, then he noticed me standing at the door.

"You too, pumpkin," he said, squeezing my shoulder gently as he walked past. I wish he would quit calling me that. I'm twelve . . . I didn't think you were allowed to call anyone over the age of ten 'pumpkin'.

But I went back to bed. Mom stayed with Adrian for a few more minutes. Finally, I saw the light click off and heard Mom walk back downstairs. The house was dark once again.

A ghost, I thought. *Not only a ghost, but the same ghost I had seen.* I was sure of it. Adrian described the same thing that I had seen in the yard below. A girl wearing a dress. A girl that was glowing blue!

I needed to talk to him. I needed to know more about what he saw. I mean . . . what if it was true? What if we had ghosts living here?

I crept out of bed and slowly tip-toed out of my room and down the hall to Adrian's room. I tried to be as quiet as I could so he wouldn't think that the ghost was coming back. Then he would start screaming again and Mom and Dad would come running. Then we'd both probably get in trouble.

I stood next to his door and peered inside. *"Adrian,"* I whispered. *"It's me . . . Alex."*

Thankfully, he recognized my voice right away.

"Hey Al," he said.

"I know what you saw," I said quietly. I stepped into his room.

"You do?" he said.

"Yes. I saw her in the yard. A girl. A girl with a dress. She has two braids in her hair."

"That's her!" he whispered excitedly. "See! It *wasn't* a nightmare! You saw her, too!"

"I saw her outside in the field. She came all the way up to the yard. She was waving at me. I think she wanted me to go outside."

"What do you suppose she wants?" Adrian asked.

"I don't know. What does *any* ghost want?"

We had to think about that one. I had never seen a real live ghost before. Up until today, I had never even believed in ghosts.

But I saw this one with my own eyes. And so did Adrian. Whoever 'she' was, she was a real ghost. There was no doubt about it.

"Well, I'm going back to bed," I said. "Let's talk about this in the morning, okay?"

No answer.

"Okay, Adrian? We'll talk about this in the morning?"

Still no answer. I could see Adrian's dark

form sitting up in bed, but he wasn't speaking.

Suddenly I knew.

He was staring past me in the darkness, to afraid to speak.

I turned around.

A light blue shimmer was glowing just beyond the door!

And it was coming *closer* . . . .

8

It was the ghost. I was sure of it.

We couldn't quite see her yet, but the blue glow was growing brighter and brighter.

Soon she would be at the door!

I felt like running, but to where? If I ran out the door, I would run directly into the ghost!

I was trapped. The only thing I could do was wait. Wait and watch.

The strange blue light grew brighter.

Closer.

And closer . . . .

Suddenly, we could see her. She drifted to the open door and stopped. I say 'drifted' because she didn't seem to walk with her feet. In fact, it didn't look like her feet were moving at all! I wasn't even sure if they even touched the floor.

And she was smiling! She just stood there, looking at us. She was actually very pretty. I guess I imagined that a ghost would be all ugly and stuff, but this one wasn't. She had a nice smile and her braids rested on her shoulders. I couldn't tell for sure, but her hair looked like it might be a dark brown.

I don't know how long we stood there, just staring. Finally, it was the *ghost* who spoke!

"Hello," she said quietly.

I tried to speak, but I couldn't! I was just too afraid. I knew Adrian was, too.

"It's okay," the ghost said. *"I'm not going to hurt you."*

It took a long time, but I finally got up enough courage to say something.

"Ummmm . . . ." It was all I could say.

She laughed at me! She must've thought that it was funny that I was too afraid to talk!

"No, really," she said. "I won't hurt you. I mean it."

There was a softness in her voice that

sounded honest and sincere. I knew that she meant it, and then I was finally able to say something that actually made sense.

"Who . . . who *are* you?" I managed to stammer.

"My name is Catherine, and this is my home. Or at least, it *was* my home. It was my home until that mean old ghost moved in."

"But . . . but—" I had so many questions, I didn't know where to begin. I never thought I'd be talking to a real live ghost before . . . if there was such a thing as a 'real live' ghost!

So that's what I asked her.

"Are . . . are you *alive?*" I said.

"Of course I'm alive," Catherine answered. "Well, not alive in a sense that you think of, but yes, I am alive. See?" She reached out her arm. "Touch my hand."

Touch a ghost?!?!?!?!

"It's okay," she urged.

I reached out, but when I tried to touch her hand, my hand seemed to slip right through! But as it did, it felt very warm.

"You see?" she said. "I am here . . . just

not quite in the same dimension as you."

I guess I wasn't too sure what a 'dimension' was, but I'm pretty sure that she meant that she was *here,* but not like Adrian and I were *here.*

This was crazy!

Here I was, awake in the middle of the night, talking to a *ghost!*

"What . . . what are you doing here?" I asked. I didn't mean for the question to be rude or anything, but I wanted to know.

"Years ago," Catherine began, "we used to live here. But not long ago, a mean ghost—a poltergeist—moved in. He's been here ever since . . . and until he goes away, we can't live here."

I knew what a poltergeist was. It was what you called a 'troublesome' ghost. And this poltergeist didn't sound so nice.

"He stole your home?"

Catherine nodded. "Yes," she said. "That's exactly what happened. He's quite a problem."

I was freaking out. And I knew that

Adrian couldn't believe what he was hearing, either. Gosh—I couldn't believe what I was *seeing!*

Finally, Adrian spoke.

"You mean that we live in a haunted house?" he asked.

Catherine nodded. "Oh, it's not haunted in the way that you probably think," she said, smiling. "Many people are afraid because they think that they will be hurt. But poltergeists never harm anyone. Except—" She stopped speaking, and the smile faded from her face.

"Except?" I urged her.

"Except maybe for this one," she said, her eyes full of concern.

Suddenly I heard a gentle squeaking coming from the stairs. I looked past Catherine.

Another fuzzy blue form was coming!

9

It was coming closer and closer.

The blue form was at the top of the stairs and was coming toward Adrian's bedroom door!

Toward *us!*

I took a step back. Adrian was still crouched in bed, and he pulled the covers up over his head.

"Don't be afraid," Catherine said smiling. "It's only my brother."

The blue form came to the door, and I could make out his features. Catherine was right! He was the same size and height as she was, and he looked a lot like her. In fact —

Suddenly I knew!

"You're . . . you're *twins*," I said.

The two ghosts smiled.

"That's right," Catherine answered, nodding her head. "This is my twin brother, Caleb."

"Hi," Caleb said, waving his hand.

Twin ghosts! I'd never heard of such a thing before.

Adrian managed to peek out from beneath the sheets.

"It's all a dream," he whispered. "It's all a dream, and I'm going to wake up. I'm going to close my eyes and you're going to go away."

He closed his eyes tightly for a moment, then opened them up.

The ghosts were still here.

"What do you want from us?" I asked.

"We need your help," Caleb answered. "We need your help in getting rid of the mean poltergeist that took our home."

"You mean that this . . . *poltergeist* . . . is living here? In *our* house?" I asked.

Catherine and Caleb nodded. "He moved in a few summers ago when Caleb and I were gone," Catherine said. "Now, he refuses to move. He thinks that this is his home."

Things began to make sense. The noises in the night, the cupboard doors opening. I mean, I guess you'd expect those things to happen if a ghost was living in your house!

"Can't you make him leave?" Adrian asked.

"No, I'm afraid not. See, he's a very different kind of ghost. We've never even seen him before."

Huh?

"You mean that even ghosts like yourselves can't see other ghosts?"

"Most times, we can," Caleb answered. "But this one stays out of sight. He can be invisible when he wants to be, so he can hide very easily."

"But . . . how can *we* help?" I asked. "We don't know a thing about ghosts."

"We'll help you," Catherine said. "But we can't do it alone. Will you please help us?"

She was serious. So was Caleb. They weren't smiling anymore. Suddenly I felt sorry for them. This was their home . . . *our* home . . . and they had been kicked out by an uninvited ghost.

And a mean one, according to Caleb and Catherine!

I turned to Adrian. He was looking at me.

"Well?" I asked.

"Well, *what?*" he answered flatly. I think he was a little freaked out over the whole thing. I guess I was, too.

I turned back around and faced Caleb and Catherine, taking a step toward them.

"We'll help," I said.

"Thank you," Catherine replied. I could tell she was very happy.

But I had no idea how much trouble we were in for!

10

Have you ever told someone that you'd do something, and later wished you'd never opened your mouth?

That's how I felt! Up until tonight, I had never even believed in ghosts . . . and here I was, telling two ghosts that I would help them! I was going to help them kick another ghost out of our house!

"Where do we start?" I asked.

"Well, first of all, you have to know what we're up against," Caleb began. "This is no ordinary poltergeist. Making him leave is going to be hard. It might even be—"

He paused, looking at his sister. "—It might even be *dangerous*," he finished. "This ghost won't listen to us. He won't leave . . . and things might get pretty tricky."

"Where is he now?" I asked.

"We never know for sure," Catherine replied. "We can sense when he's around, but we can't see him. We only know when he's near."

"He's not near now, is he?" Adrian asked.

"No," Catherine said. "But he'll probably return soon."

"How do *we* know when he's around?" I asked.

"Oh, you'll know, all right," Caleb replied. "He creates a lot of mischief. He slams doors, leaves doors open. Stuff like that."

"Hey!" I exclaimed. "Maybe that was who left the cupboard doors open! And the glass of water on the counter!"

"Well, partly," Catherine said. "The open cupboards were from the mean ghost. The glass of water was from *me*. I put the water there to try and get your attention. But every time I tried, that mean poltergeist showed up, and I had to leave."

So that was the answer! Catherine was

the one filling up the glass of ice water in the middle of the night!

"When do we start?" I asked. "What do we need to do?" I had so many questions.

"Not tonight," Catherine replied. "He'll be back soon. We don't have any time tonight."

"Let's start tomorrow," Caleb chimed in. "There's a big old maple tree on the far side of the field. Do you know the one?"

Both Adrian and I nodded. It was a huge tree, with a giant trunk. Once Adrian climbed up it.

"Good," Caleb answered. "Meet us there tomorrow evening. We'll have more time to make plans." He stopped speaking, and the two shimmering ghosts looked at each other.

"Are you going to tell them, or should I?" Catherine asked.

Caleb frowned. "I will," he said. He looked at Adrian and I. "Whatever you do, don't *ever* go down into the cellar. Stay away from the cellar until we can get that ghost out of here."

"Why?" I asked. "I've been in the cellar dozens of times . . . so has Adrian. Mom and

Dad have a lot of stuff stored there."

"You mustn't go down there," was all he said. "Stay away from the cellar. Stay away and —"

"*Caleb!*" Catherine suddenly hissed. "*He's coming!! He's coming back!*"

The twin ghosts suddenly looked very alarmed.

"We have to leave," Catherine said.

They started to fade away!

"Where are you going?" I asked frantically. I mean . . . I didn't want to be left all alone to face a mean poltergeist!

"Tomorrow evening," Catherine said. She and Caleb were fading quickly now. They were disappearing! There wasn't much left of the ghosts except a hazy mist. But I could hear Catherine's voice as she faded away.

"*Tomorrow evening,*" she was saying. "*Tomorrow evening by the old tree . . . .*"

And then she and Caleb were gone.

They were gone, and Adrian and I were alone. Well, not alone, exactly.

Down the hall we heard the floor squeaking. It sounded like slow-moving footsteps.

The mean poltergeist had returned.

"What do we do now?" I whispered.

Adrian just shook his head and pulled his covers up over his eyes.

What a chicken! Some brother he is, leaving me all alone to fend for myself.

There was more squeaking from outside the door. Whoever . . . or *whatever* . . . was almost here.

Suddenly the door began to move! It began to close, very slowly.

Then it stopped. I could hear footsteps walking away. Everything was quiet again.

I stood in Adrian's room for a long time, too frightened to move, wondering what to do next.

"Adrian?" I whispered.

No answer.

"Adrian . . . ." A bit louder. I turned.

He was sleeping! He had fallen back to sleep. I was a little tired, too, so I gathered up my courage and slowly began walking.

I stopped at the door and peered around the corner. It was still very dark, and all I could see were shadows.

But no poltergeist! That was a relief.

I stood at the door a moment and then walked down the hall. I passed the staircase, tip-toeing as softly as I could. Still, the old boards beneath my feet cried out as I walked.

Finally, I made it to my room. I climbed back into bed, pulled the covers up to my chin, and fell asleep.

I awoke the next morning to the sounds of chirping birds and a lawnmower. It was Saturday, and Dad was cutting the grass, just like he does every Saturday morning. I wish he wouldn't do it so early, though. The noisy lawnmower always wakes me up.

I got up, dressed, and went downstairs. Adrian was already up, and he sat at the counter, sipping on a glass of apple juice and eating a slice of toast. I sat down next to him.

"G'morning, Mom," I said sleepily.

"Good morning, sweetheart," she said, handing me a glass of orange juice. She looked at me. "Are you feeling okay?" she asked. "You look tired."

"I didn't sleep very well last night," I said.

Beneath the counter, Adrian gently nudged me with his leg.

"Well, one of you didn't sleep much last night," Mom replied. "Which one of you came down here and opened all of the drawers and cupboards again?"

12

Saturday morning is a busy place at our house. Adrian and I each have a huge amount of chores to do. Actually, we *all* do a lot of work. Saturday is the day that Dad spends working around the yard. Mom works around the house, and Adrian and I do a lot of different things.

First, we have to clean our rooms. Then, depending on how much work needs to be done, we help Mom or Dad. We all work pretty hard until about noon, and then we have a big lunch. Sometimes we go to a restaurant in Petoskey. My favorite food is Chinese. The only thing Adrian likes are hamburgers.

Today we had a lot of things to do. I raked the yard, and Adrian helped Dad cut up wood from a tree that had fallen down not far from our house. They cut and stacked the wood. We'll burn it in our fireplace during the winter.

I was busy inside with Mom all morning. Living in such a big, old house takes a lot of work. It took me almost an hour just to vacuum upstairs!

Then I went outside to help Dad. We had to clean up all of the tree branches from the fallen tree, and haul the limbs over into the woods. Adrian came and helped, and we finished the job quickly.

Dad was in the garage looking for something when Adrian came up to me in the yard. We hadn't had a chance to talk about what had happened last night.

"See anymore of . . . ." His voice just kind of faded off. I think he was going to say 'the ghosts' or something like that.

I just shook my head. "That was so weird," I said. "But I guess that explains why the cupboards keep opening by themselves. Or *seem* to open by themselves. Now we know that something else is doing it."

"Do you think that the poltergeist is really

dangerous?" Adrian asked.

I shook my head. "I don't know," I answered. "But we'd just better do what Caleb and Catherine ask us to do. They really seemed frightened by this mean ghost."

Dad called out to Adrian, and I didn't get a chance to talk with him about the ghosts anymore. I went back inside to finish helping Mom in the house.

I was washing the dishes in the kitchen when she called out from the living room.

"Sweetheart . . . can you run down to the cellar and get me the broom?"

Gulp.

Double gulp.

Triple gulp.

Caleb had told us last night to never, *ever*, go down to the cellar again.

What was I going to do? There was no way that Mom would believe me if I told her about Catherine and Caleb.

And the two ghosts were very strict with their warning: *Don't go into the cellar.*

But what about Mom and Dad? Did that mean them, too? I hadn't had a chance to ask that question.

What was so bad about the cellar that Catherine and Caleb didn't want us to go down there?

I thought about it. I've been in the cellar before. Nothing's happened. Nothing out of the ordinary, anyway.

Should I take a chance?

"Sweetheart?" Mom called out again.

"Okay, Mom," I answered. I decided that I would go down into the cellar.

I dried off my hands and walked down the hall. The floor creaked beneath my sneakers.

Creak . . . creak . . . creak . . . .

The door of the cellar is small . . . so small that even I have to duck down. It's made out of old wood and has a deadbolt to keep it closed.

I reached out to open the door. I could still hear Caleb's words last night, telling me to never go into the cellar.

I paused for just a moment, listening. There was nothing to hear except the shuffling of Mom's feet in the living room.

I grasped the bolt and slid it over to the side, and the door slowly chugged open.

13

There are no lights in the cellar. Dad says he is going to put some in, but he hasn't yet. On the wall near the door of the cellar is a big flashlight . . . you know the kind. The ones that take those big, square batteries. Lantern batteries is what they're called, I think.

I reached over, picked up the flashlight, and clicked it on.

Never, ever go down into the cellar.

The words of Caleb spun around in my head.

Never, ever go down into the cellar.

I placed my foot on the first step, aiming the flashlight beam down into the darkness. The air was dry and dusty.

Another step.

Never, ever go down into the cellar.

One more step.

I turned and looked back behind me. I had only taken two steps down, so I was still right at the doorway of the cellar, still at the top of the stairs. Outside, I heard the chainsaw start up. Dad was probably trimming some more branches. I turned back around, and looked down the dark staircase.

There was something there! Or, rather, there *had* been something there! In the beam of light! It was like a shadow, a form of some sort. When I had turned back around, it quickly disappeared.

What was it? What had it been?

I was terrified. I didn't breathe. I didn't move. I just froze, standing on the second step, peering down into the dark cellar. I thought I could hear a noise coming from somewhere in the darkness, but I couldn't be sure.

Never, ever go down into the cellar. It was as if Caleb was inside my head. I could hear his voice louder now, more insistent, warning me.

Never, ever go down into the cellar . . . Never,

ever go down into the cellar . . . Never —

A face! Suddenly, a face appeared in the flashlight beam! It was very faint, but there was no mistake—it was a face.

But . . . a face of *what?*

It didn't look like a human face, but, then again, it didn't look like an animal's face, either. It was just a pair of eyes and a wide, toothy mouth. And a nose. The face seemed to change even as I watched it. The eyes grew larger, then smaller. The mouth changed from a smile to a snarl, and the nose twitched back and forth.

I could feel my heart pounding in my chest, and I thought that it was about to explode. I wanted to run, but I was too afraid.

Then . . . a *hand!* I could see a hand in the darkness, reaching for me, urging me down the steps.

Right! Like I was going to go down into the cellar *now!*

I was just about to turn and bolt when I heard a loud thud and a heavy click behind me.

Oh no!

The door had slammed shut! I was trapped in the cellar!

14

I screamed at the very top of my lungs.

Then I screamed again. And again.

The door suddenly swung open! Mom was standing there!

"For heaven's sake, Alex," she said. "I accidentally bumped into the door and it closed. That's no reason to scream like that."

"But Mom!" I began, brushing past her. "I saw something down there! There was something there!" I pointed the flashlight down into the darkness.

There was nothing there.

"What did you see?" Mom asked.

"I . . . I don't know for sure," I stammered. "But there was something there."

We both stood there a moment, staring down into the cellar.

"Well, whatever it was, it's gone now. Probably just a mouse. Oh . . . never mind the broom. I found one in the foyer." She closed the cellar door.

That had been a close one! Never again would I doubt what Caleb and Catherine told me.

When we finished our work, Dad told us that we would be having lunch in Petoskey. Cool! That usually means that we go shopping, too.

After lunch we walked downtown. Dad and Adrian played frisbee in Pennsylvania Park. Mom and I went shopping at some of the stores on Mitchell Street.

I had fun, but I was feeling very anxious. I still hadn't had a chance to tell Adrian about what I saw in the cellar. Plus, as the afternoon wore on, I knew it was only going to be a matter of time. Soon, we would be meeting Catherine and Caleb out by the old maple tree.

Then what? What, exactly, did they want us to do? How were we going to help them get rid of that mean ghost?

When we finished shopping, we met up with Dad and Adrian in the park. Then we walked through a small tunnel that goes under US-31. The tunnel opens up right near the bay! Today it was sunny and warm, and we walked along the docks, looking at the beautiful boats. When Mom and Dad sat down on a bench, Adrian and I took a walk along the breakwall. Finally, we had a chance to be alone.

"You're not going to believe what I saw in the cellar," I said as our tennis shoes padded the cement breakwall. A few seagulls screeched and wheeled in the blue sky above.

"What?!?!" he exclaimed. "You went into the cellar?!? Caleb told us never to go there!!"

"I had to," I explained. "Mom asked me to get a broom, so I *had* to go down there."

But then I told him that I hadn't actually gone *down* into the cellar, but just stood at the top of the stairs. I told him about the face and the eyes and the mouth and the hands.

"Wow," he said. "That's freaky."

"You're telling me," I said, nodding. "It was spooky. Worse. It was super-spooky."

We didn't talk about it anymore. We were both a bit nervous, I think. Nervous about our meeting with Caleb and Catherine.

And nervous about the house, too. We had started to realize that we were living in an honest-to-goodness 'haunted' house!

It was late in the day. We made one stop on the way home so Dad could fill the car with gas. Mom said that we would be having a late dinner, and that they would be having some guests over. Some of the people that Dad works with, she told us. But until then, we could do what we wanted.

Which would work out perfect. We would be meeting Caleb and Catherine just as the sun was going down, and we'd have about an hour before dinner time.

That evening, I went to Adrian's room and knocked on the door.

"Come in," he said. He was sprawled out on his stomach on the bed, flipping through a comic book.

"Ready?" I asked.

He closed his comic book. "About as ready as I'll ever be," he said, standing up.

"Let's go."

Our meeting with Caleb and Catherine was about to start. Little did I know that the real terror was about to begin.

15

We walked across the field through the tall grass. The old maple tree is a long ways off, and we can just barely see it from our house. It would take a few minutes to get there.

The setting sun was beautiful! The bright yellow ball dipped below the trees, and, as it did, a few clouds reflected pretty shades of red and orange and pink. I think Petoskey has the most beautiful sunsets in the world.

But the setting sun also meant something else:

Darkness.

When our meeting with Caleb and Catherine was over, we would be walking back to the house in total darkness.

Adrian brought a small flashlight, so *that* would help. We would be able to see the lights of the house, even from the old maple tree, so we wouldn't get lost.

But I just felt kind of weird . . . maybe even a bit scared . . . now that I knew there might be ghosts around. Ghosts besides Caleb and Catherine, anyway.

We finally reached the tree. There was still enough light to see, but it was growing dark quickly. There was no sign of Caleb or Catherine.

"I wonder where they are?" Adrian asked.

He had just spoken those words when I began to see a faint blue glow through the woods.

"Adrian . . . *look.*" Adrian turned to see for himself.

The blue image was growing brighter as it came closer. Then there were two!

Caleb and Catherine!

"Hi guys," Caleb said as he reached the tree.

"Hi" Adrian and I said.

"Sorry we're late," Catherine apologized.

"That's okay," I said. It was still kind of shocking when I thought about it . . . standing next to an old tree, talking with two *ghosts!*

But I had to tell them something. I had to tell them about the cellar. I didn't want to say anything, since they had warned me not to go there. But I had to know what it was that I saw. Maybe Caleb or Catherine knew.

"I have something to tell you," I began sheepishly. "I . . . I know you told us never to go into the cellar . . . but . . . well, I did. Earlier today."

Silence. Catherine and Caleb only stared at me.

Finally, Catherine spoke. "You . . . you *what?*" she said, her mouth open wide.

"I went into the cellar. Not all the way down, only to the second step."

Catherine looked at Caleb. They both looked very concerned.

"Think very hard," Caleb said calmly. "Did you see anything?"

"Yes," I said. "Yes, I did. I mean . . . I *think* I did."

Once again, Catherine and Caleb

exchanged nervous glances.

"What did you see?" Catherine asked.

"Well, I can't be sure. But, it looked like a face of some sort. It was really weird. I've never seen anything like it before. Ever."

"Oh no!" Catherine suddenly cried out. "It was *him!* You saw *him!*" I thought she was going to cry! She was very upset.

And I was getting upset, too! I was getting worried just looking at how worried Catherine and Caleb were!

"Now we *do* have a big problem," Caleb said. "I think we'd all better sit down."

We all sat cross-legged next to the old maple, and Caleb began.

"What you saw," he said, "was the mean ghost that moved in and took our place. Normally, people can't see ghosts. However, we had told you about him the night before. That means that you *believed*. You believed that he was there."

"What's so bad about that?" Adrian asked.

"The problem with that," Caleb said quietly, "is that now that you have seen him, you have entered his world."

I still didn't understand all this. It was so confusing.

"It will happen," Catherine added sadly. "It's just a matter of time. But it *will* happen."

"*What* will happen?" I asked.

Caleb took a deep breath, let it out, and looked at me. His face was serious. *"Alex,"* he said, *"you are going to become a ghost."*

16

Oh no!

I think I was prepared to hear anything—except that!

"A *ghost!?!?!*" I cried. "You mean . . . I'm going to be *ghost?!?!* Like you are?!?!"

Both Caleb and Catherine nodded their heads. Adrian looked horrified! He just stared at me, his mouth open, eyes wide.

"But . . . but . . . I *can't* be a ghost! I just can't be! School is going to start soon . . . I have stuff to do! What's Mom and Dad going to say?"

"They won't see you," Catherine replied. "You'll be invisible. The only ones who can see you will be Caleb and I. And Adrian. Soon, you will look just like we do."

"You mean . . . kind of like blue and misty and glowing?" Adrian asked.

"Yes," Caleb replied. "I'm afraid so."

"Isn't there any way to change back?" I asked frantically. "Can't I reverse it or something?"

"The only way to reverse it is to remove the ghost by the stroke of midnight on the day that you saw him. That would be midnight tonight. And there's no way we'll have the time to get that ghost out of there. He's a mean ghost, and he wants to stay in your house."

"But we have to try!" I cried. "We have to!" I started to cry a tiny bit.

Caleb and Catherine looked at one another.

"We can try," Catherine whispered. "We can try. But I don't know if it'll work. There's not much time."

"Well, what do we have to do?" I asked, jumping to my feet. I mean . . . there wasn't a minute to spare! I didn't want to be a ghost for the rest of my life! And how would Mom and Dad feel . . . having a ghost for a daughter?!? I'd be grounded. I'd be the only grounded ghost on the planet.

"Alex! Look!" Adrian pointed at my hand.

Oh no! It was happening! It was happening already!

My hand was turning a faint powder-blue. And it seemed to be glowing.

I was turning into a ghost!

I looked at my other hand. It, too, was turning a faint, misty blue.

"What do I do?!?!" I cried. "What do I do!?!?!"

"There's nothing you can do, Alex," Caleb replied, shaking his head. "You can't stop it. The only thing we can do is try and get that ghost out of your house by midnight. If we can't do that, well . . . ." He stopped.

"Well what?" I asked.

"Then you'll be a ghost. *Forever*. You'll be a ghost—*just like us* . . . ."

17

Why didn't I listen to what Caleb told me about the cellar? If I would have only listened, I wouldn't be in this mess.

"How long will it take before I'm a . . . a *ghost?*" I managed to stammer.

"Not long, now," said Catherine. "Once it starts . . . there's nothing you can do to stop it."

And she was right.

Soon my whole body was a brilliant, shimmering blue. Even Adrian was freaked out! He looked at me like I was . . . well . . . a *ghost.*

"There's not much time," Catherine said. "We have to get started."

"But what do we have to do?" Adrian

asked.

"First thing, we have to go back to the house," answered Caleb.

"What?!?!" I cried. "I can't go back to the house! Not like this!"

Catherine managed a laugh. "No one will see you," she said. "You're invisible. Just like us. The only people who can see us is you two, and that's because we chose for you to see us."

"Can I 'choose' for Mom and Dad to see me?" I asked.

"Sure," Catherine said. "But I don't think you'll want them to see you. It would be pretty hard to explain later, if—I mean *when*—you change back."

Great. I was in deep trouble.

But, I did have to admit, it might be fun to be invisible . . . at least for a little while.

"Come on," Caleb said. "We've got to get to work."

And so we started back through the field. It was really strange to look down at myself and see my whole body—my clothes and everything—glowing blue!

By now it was completely dark. We

walked up behind our shed and stopped.

Suddenly, another thought occurred to me. What was I going to do about dinner? I couldn't go into the house like this! I mean . . . I guess I *could,* but if Mom and Dad couldn't see me, they'd wonder where I was.

"Adrian," I said. "How are we — how are *you* — going to explain this to Mom and Dad? What are they going to say if I'm not there for dinner?"

Adrian scratched his head. "Gosh, I hadn't thought of that, Al," he said. Caleb and Catherine didn't have any ideas, either.

Suddenly, I had a plan!

"Hey!" I said. "Stacey's house! Tell Mom and Dad that I'm at Stacey's house having dinner!"

"Great idea!" Adrian said. "That'll work!" And I knew it would. Stacey and I are best friends. We spend a lot of time together — and we eat at each others' houses often. Mom and Dad wouldn't suspect anything!

So we had one problem solved.

"I'm going to go in," Adrian said. "It'll be time for dinner soon."

"We're going to need your help," Caleb said. "Can you meet us right back here at the shed in an hour?"

"Sure," Adrian answered, and he ran to the porch, and went in the house.

"Well," I said. "What now?"

"Now," Catherine said, "we go into the cellar."

18

That was the last thing I wanted to hear.

"The *cellar?!?!?*" I exclaimed. "You've got to be kidding!! You told me never to go in there!"

"Yeah, and a lot of good it did," Caleb smirked.

Well, I guess I deserved that one.

"But what's the plan? I mean . . . what are we going to do? How do we get the poltergeist out?"

"It won't be easy," Catherine said. "He's a very mischievous ghost."

"And besides," Caleb spoke up, "getting him out won't necessarily be the hard part. Keeping him from coming back will probably be the most difficult."

"What will we do when we get to the cellar?" I asked. "If he's such a mean poltergeist, won't he be mad?"

"Chances are, he's gone right now," Catherine said. "He usually leaves at night. Or he spends the time wandering around the house."

I shuddered at the thought of a mean ghost wandering around the house . . . *my house!*

I looked around the night sky. The moon shined brightly. The sky was filled with millions of stars. The crickets were singing, and every once in a while I could hear the high-pitched squeak of a bat as it spun through the air in search of bugs.

"Let's go," Caleb said, and he began to drift toward the house. And when I say 'drift' I mean *drift.* I guess I hadn't noticed it until now, but that's how he was moving around. It was like his feet never even moved!

"Hey!" I said. "Can I do that?"

"Sure," Caleb replied, floating back to me. His feet were a few inches off the ground! He was really floating!

Well, I guess that's not too surprising. After all — he is a *ghost*.

"Just think about walking without moving your feet," he explained. "It's as easy as that."

And it was! When I thought about it, my feet came right up off the ground a few inches! Then when I thought about walking, I just kind of 'drifted' along!

Maybe being a ghost wasn't going to be so bad after all!

But then I thought about it again. While it *might* be fun to be a ghost for a *little* while, I did *not* want to be a ghost for the rest of my life.

The three of us drifted to the front door of our house. I reached forward to open the door, but Catherine stopped me.

"No," she said. "Someone might see the door open. Even though your Mom and Dad can't see us, they can see things move if we move them. Watch — there's an easier way."

And with that, Catherine slipped right through the door! She went right into the door and vanished!

"Come on," Caleb said, taking my hand. "It's easy."

Suddenly I was going through the door! It was a really weird feeling. It was very dark for just a second . . . and then I was inside our house.

As we drifted by the kitchen, I saw Mom and Dad and Adrian at the table. Adrian saw us, and his jaw dropped. His eyes grew wide and he stopped eating. He looked like he had seen . . . well . . . a *ghost!* I guess we surprised him.

All of a sudden, Mom and Dad turned! They had caught Adrian's shocked expression and had turned to see what he was looking at!

Could they see us?!?!?

19

"Don't worry," Catherine said. "They can't see us or hear us."

I hoped she was right

"What did you see, Adrian?" Mom asked.

"Oh . . . ah . . . nothing, Mom. I guess I thought I saw . . . a *moth*. Yeah. But it was nothing."

"That's good," Mom said. "I don't want any moths in here." Mom and Dad turned back around and continued eating.

Caleb and Catherine were right! Mom and Dad really couldn't see us! Adrian could, but to Mom and Dad . . . we were completely invisible!

Catherine began drifting again, and Caleb

and I drifted along behind her. We stopped at the door to the cellar.

All of a sudden I was very frightened. This was all too new, too weird. I didn't think I wanted to confront a mean poltergeist. Caleb and Catherine were poltergeists, but they were different. They were nice poltergeists. The one that lived in the cellar was mean.

"How are we going to get rid of him?" I asked. I was clueless. For all I knew, we might have to cast a spell on him.

"Well, I guess we'd better explain before we go any further," Caleb said.

Catherine spoke up. "What we have to do is find him another home. We have to find a home for him that he willingly wants to live in. If we find him a new home, then we can move back in . . . and you won't be a ghost anymore."

"We have to do this by midnight?" I asked.

Caleb and Catherine nodded. "That's the problem. We have to find him and confront him."

"You mean . . . we have to *ask* him to leave?" I asked. That seemed crazy. I didn't want to ask a mean ghost to do anything . . . besides leave me alone.

"Well, that's the first step," Caleb said.

"What if he doesn't want to leave?" I asked.

Once again, Caleb and Catherine exchanged nervous glances.

"If we can't get him to leave tonight, there are other ways . . . but by then it'll be too late. You'll still be a ghost."

Gulp.

"Okay," Catherine said. "Here's the plan. I'll sneak down to the cellar to see if he's there. You two wait right here, and I'll be right back."

In the next instant, Catherine had slipped right through the cellar door. She was gone.

"What do we do?" I asked Caleb.

"We wait. We wait for Catherine to come back."

It seemed to take forever. I don't know how long we stood there, standing in front of the door.

We got a surprise when Dad suddenly appeared and walked right past us! He was going to the garage to get something, and he came back again. It was kind of funny! Here we were, just a few feet from him, but he couldn't see us!

I could hear the dinner dishes clanging in the sink, and I knew that Adrian was helping Mom in the kitchen. We both have things that we have to do after a meal . . . this week it was Adrian's turn to wash dishes. I could hear Mom and Dad picking up the house and getting ready for their guests to arrive. I'm sure it wouldn't be long before they started showing up.

Suddenly Catherine appeared, a shimmering blue form that came right through the cellar door.

"He's there," she said.

"Did he see you?" Caleb asked.

"No, he didn't," Catherine replied. "He was sleeping."

A sleeping ghost? That was a surprise. I guess I just thought all ghosts stayed awake all the time.

"Let's go," Caleb said, taking my hand. Catherine took the other, and the three of us slipped silently through the door.

We were going down into the cellar.

20

Going down into the cellar was spooky. I could see Caleb and Catherine, and even *myself*, glowing faintly in the darkness. But we hardly gave off any real 'light', and the cellar was very dark.

Except . . . .

Except in the far corner of the cellar, there was another faint blue glow.

The mean poltergeist!

We stopped at the bottom of the stairs. Now I was *scared*. If it hadn't been for Caleb and Catherine, I would have run away right then and there.

But they squeezed my hands to let me know everything was okay. I *hoped* everything would be okay, anyway.

"Don't worry," Catherine whispered quietly. But I could tell that even *she* was a little bit afraid. I was sure that they don't encounter ghosts like this too often. And there was something that had made them afraid of this particular ghost, because they had never confronted him before.

But now we had to. We had to, because it was the only way that I would be able to turn back into a normal human!

I didn't want to be a ghost for the rest of my life. I wanted to play and ride horses with Stacey and go to school and college. I wanted to go swimming. I wanted to have fun with friends.

I did NOT want to be a ghost!

Slowly, very slowly, we began to drift toward the sleeping ghost. As we drew closer, I could hear a noise. It was a quiet rumble, and I didn't know what it was.

Then I knew! As we approached the sleeping poltergeist, the rumble grew louder.

He was snoring! A snoring ghost!

Now I've seen everything!

But let me describe the ghost . . . because that was the strangest part of all!

First of all, I must say that I expected him to be like some scary monster with ugly teeth and big eyes and a nasty grin—but he wasn't like that at all! He looked like any normal man would look like. He had short hair (I couldn't really tell what color, because he was glowing blue!) and was wearing what appeared to be an old coat. He wore slacks and a pair of boots. If he hadn't been glowing blue like he was, he would have looked just like any normal man would look like.

Except, of course, he was sleeping on the floor!

We stood over him, watching him sleep. I could hear my heart pounding in my chest, and I wondered if Caleb and Catherine could hear it, too.

Tha-thump . . . tha-thump . . . tha-thump . . .

.

What was going to happen now? What if the ghost woke up? What would he do?

We were about to find out!

21

Caleb leaned over the ghost. "Excuse me," he said.

The poltergeist opened his eyes! For a moment he looked like he was going to go back to sleep, and then he suddenly realized that there were three ghosts standing around him! His eyes snapped open wide.

We sure must have surprised him, because he immediately shot up from where he had been sleeping and flew across the room!

"Get away from me!" he yelled. "Stay away! I'm warning you!"

We didn't say a word. He looked more frightened than we did!

Suddenly his face began to change! Fangs

began to grow out of his mouth, his eyes grew bigger . . . his whole body even grew bigger!

Then I recognized him! That was the exact same face that I had seen when I stood at the top of the cellar, staring down!

He was scary. Scary and ugly-looking. I began to back away, but Catherine squeezed my hand harder.

"Don't worry," she said. "It's all an act. He's just trying to scare us."

In the next instant, the ghost was gone! He just sort of zipped straight up through the ceiling! The ghost had gone upstairs into the house!

Caleb, Catherine and I floated upstairs and through the door. We hurried down the hall.

There were all kinds of loud noises coming from the kitchen! I could hear banging and pounding and the slamming of doors.

When we rounded the corner, it was exactly as I thought. The mean ghost was rushing around the kitchen, opening cupboard doors and slamming them closed! Adrian was backed into a corner, horrified. He could see the ghost whirling about, bumping into things, making a terrible racket.

From the second floor, I heard Mom call out. "What on earth are you doing down there?" she hollered.

Adrian, trying to be as calm as he could, shouted back. "Ummm . . . just putting the . . . the dishes away," he hollered. His voice was shaking.

"Well, quit making so much noise! There's no reason to make such a racket!"

Suddenly the mischievous ghost grabbed a plate and flung it into the air!

Oh no!

Quick as lightning, Adrian dove forward to try and catch the plate. His hands were stretched out as far as they could, but the plate was falling, *falling* . . . .

He caught it! Adrian fumbled the plate in his hands, but he caught it only inches before it hit the floor! He stood back up and set it on the counter.

The ghost, seeing that this might be fun, picked up another plate and launched it. Again, Adrian was flying through the air, in a desperate attempt to save the plate! It was horrible! If he dropped one, it would shatter for sure.

How would he explain *that* to Mom and Dad?

Luckily, he caught the plate. He set it down and turned back around, waiting for the ghost to throw another one.

But the ghost must have become bored. He threw his head back, laughed, and disappeared through the floor.

"Come on!" Caleb said quickly. "Back to the cellar!"

I was about to float over to the cellar door when Catherine grabbed my hand again and we sank straight into the floor! We actually went right through the floor and down to the cellar!

On the other side of the room, the poltergeist stood facing us, looking as nasty and ugly as ever.

I don't know why, but suddenly I became angry. The more I thought about it, the angrier I became!

This was *my* house. *Our* house. What right did a poltergeist have trying to scare us like this?!?! We never did anything to him. I felt like marching right up to him and giving him a piece of my mind.

And so I DID! I floated right over to him and stood right in his face.

Boy was he ugly! Even uglier than I thought.

"Knock it off!" I yelled. "You don't scare me one bit, you big meanie!"

He stopped moving and stared at me.

Then something really strange began to happen. His face began to change again. It twisted and turned, and his fangs went away. His face returned to a normal size, and soon he looked just like a man again.

Well, a *ghost* anyway!

"You should be ashamed of yourself!" I said sternly. I was really mad now! "Scaring my two friends like you have! And kicking them out of their own home. Don't you have any manners at all?"

Suddenly, the ghost looked sad. He hung his head and he looked down at the ground. I think that he was actually ashamed of himself!

"I'm sorry," he said. He looked up at me, and then at Caleb and Catherine. "I just wanted a place to live. A place where no one would bother me. When I found this place, I thought it would be perfect. I'm so tired of moving from house to house, only to have people move in and change everything around."

"But why do you have to scare people?" I demanded angrily.

"I . . . I don't mean to," he said. "I just want a place with some peace and quiet. A place of my own where I can live without anyone making all kinds of noise."

"Well, it's not right that you kicked out my friends," I said. I wasn't as angry now. In fact, I started to feel a bit sorry for him.

But then I remembered . . . I had a real problem. The only way I could return to being a real person was by getting the ghost to agree to move out and find another home.

How were we going to be able to do that—*by midnight tonight?*

22

Caleb and Catherine floated up next to us.

Suddenly the ghost recognized me! "Hey," he said . . . "I thought you were a *ghost!* But you're not! You're the girl that lives in this house!"

"That's right," Caleb said. "And it's because of you that she *is* a ghost! This is *your fault!*"

"Oh dear," the poltergeist said. "That *is* a problem. That is a *terrible* problem."

"Well, we can stand here and talk about problems all night, and that won't help," Catherine said. "We have until midnight. If you don't find a new home by then—"

"—then you'll be a ghost forever," the

poltergeist said, looking at me. He really did look like he was sorry. "But how am I going to find a new place by midnight?"

"We'll help you," Caleb said. "We'll help you look, but you have to promise never to come back here and bother anyone again."

"I promise," he said. "Let's get started."

"Umm, this might be a dumb question," I began, "but how do we go about finding a new home? I mean, can't you just go down the street until you come to the next house? Can't you live there?"

"I'm afraid it isn't that simple," the poltergeist said. "You see, many, many homes are already being used by ghosts. I have to find one of my own, just like your family had to find a house of their own."

Upstairs, I heard the grandfather clock chime.

Nine o'clock. We had three hours.

"We'd better get started," Caleb said. "Let's split up into pairs."

"Wait," Catherine said. She looked at the ghost. "We don't even know your name."

The ghost smiled and bowed a tiny bit.

"Robert," he said. "At your service."

A poltergeist named Robert.

"I'm—" I was about to introduce myself and Caleb and Catherine, but he held up his hand.

"You're Alex. Your brother Adrian is upstairs."

I was surprised that he knew who we were, but then I smiled. He lived here, too. Of course he would know our names! And the names of Caleb and Catherine as well, being that he was the one who kicked them out.

"What about Adrian?" I asked. "We're supposed to meet him by the shed."

"Oh, I almost forgot!" said Caleb, smacking his forehead with his hand. "Let's go."

The four of us drifted up the stairs and through the cellar door. In the foyer, there were three adults that I didn't recognize. I think they were friends from Dad's work. I was startled to see them, and again I wondered if they could see us. Apparently not, for we just floated right on by, through the wall, and outside. They never saw us!

Adrian was waiting for us behind the shed. He was surprised to see four glowing figures coming his way, and not just three as he'd expected.

"Adrian, this is Robert," I said. Adrian was wary, and Robert spoke up.

"I was the one tossing the plates at you, an action which I am deeply sorry about." He bowed his head.

"That was *you?*" Adrian said. "It didn't look like you at all!"

"Well," Robert replied, "did I look like *this?*"

Suddenly Robert's face began to change. His fangs came back and he looked as ugly as ever. Adrian took a few steps back.

"That *was* you?!?!?" he cried. "*You* were the one throwing the plates?!?!?!?!"

"And I must say," Robert said, nodding as he spoke, "you did a great job of catching them all. I would look into a career in football or baseball if I were you."

I laughed at that. Adrian? Playing football? Hardly. *I* can throw a football better than *he* can!

"Well, thanks," Adrian said, thanking Robert for the compliment. "Thanks . . . I *think*."

"Thanks for what?"

We all turned, because the voice didn't come from any of us that were standing by the shed . . . it came from the driveway!

There was someone standing there, looking at us!

23

Dad!

He was standing in the driveway! Even though it was dark, the porch light gave off enough glow for us to see him.

Question was . . . could he see *us?*

"Thanks for what?" Dad asked again. He must be talking to Adrian!

"Uh, thanks for . . . for ummm . . . for being a great guy."

"You're welcome," Dad replied. "What are you doing back there all by yourself?" He started walking toward us—but at least I knew that he couldn't see us! He must've heard Adrian's voice, but not ours.

"Oh, uh . . . it was a toad. I saw him hop

over here. I was trying to catch him." At this, Adrian dropped down on his hands and knees, pretending to look for the toad in the darkness. He looked pretty silly.

"Well, don't stay out here too late. And remember . . . we have guests in the house. If you catch that toad, I do *not* want to see him in the house. Your mother would have a fit."

"Sure thing, Dad," Adrian said. He was still hopping around on his hands and knees, acting like he was chasing the toad! It was really quite funny.

Dad turned and walked back to the house. "And don't stay out too late," he called back.

"Don't worry, I wont," Adrian shouted.

After Dad was in the house, Adrian spoke again. "That was a close one," he said, bounding back to his feet.

And it was. Adrian could be seen . . . but Caleb, Catherine, Robert, and myself were invisible. We'd have to be careful . . . but especially Adrian. He'd have to be *really* careful.

We filled him in on what we were going to do, then we split up into two groups. Adrian, Catherine and Robert in one, and Caleb and I in the other.

"We'll need to start by searching the houses on this street," Caleb said. "Alex and I will go up this way—" he pointed with his finger—"and you guys go that way." He swung his arm back around and pointed in the opposite direction.

"What do you mean 'search' the houses?" I asked.

"Find out if there's any ghosts living in any of them," Caleb replied. "We have to search all the houses—the abandoned ones, mostly—to see if any are already haunted. If we can find one that's not, then we're in business."

Great. We were going ghost-hunting.

The serious trouble was about to begin.

24

Nine thirty.

In two and a half hours, if we hadn't found a home for Robert, I would be a ghost.

Forever.

"Who makes up these dumb ghost rules," I grumbled to Caleb. We were walking along a dirt road in the darkness, looking for old, abandoned houses. So far, we hadn't had much luck.

"What do you mean by 'rules?'" Caleb asked.

"Oh, you know. Like . . . why was I turned into a ghost when I saw Robert in the cellar? How come we have to find him a place by midnight? I mean . . . *he* was the one who caused all these problems in the first place."

"With a little help from you," Caleb answered. "We warned you about going into the cellar."

Whoops. He was right. I guess this whole mess was partly my fault, too.

The night air was fresh and clean, and a chorus of crickets sang to us as we made our way down a lonely, dark road. So far, we hadn't come across very many houses at all.

"Can't we just find an old shed or a barn or something?" I asked.

"What would he do in the winter?" was Caleb's response. "Ghosts get cold, too, you know."

You learn something new every day.

We walked and walked and walked and walked. Actually, we just drifted, but it seemed like we were walking. We must have drifted for miles! And all this time I just kept hoping that Robert, Catherine, and Adrian were having better luck than we were.

Suddenly Caleb stopped, grabbing my arm.

"Look," he said, pointing to the forest.

I strained my eyes and squinted to see what he was looking at. It was very dark, and I couldn't see anything.

"What is it?" I asked.

"I'm not sure," Caleb answered. "But it looks like a house."

Then I saw it! It was just a dark shadow of a house, far back from the road. There were no lights on. I was sure that no one was home.

"Let's go have a closer look," Caleb said.

We turned off the dirt road and found a driveway.

Soon, we stood before the house. It was huge! Much bigger than our home. And we had a pretty big house ourselves!

"What do you think?" I whispered. "Do you think there's anyone in there?"

"I'm sure that no one is in there," Caleb answered. "Question is . . . are there any poltergeists in there?"

I was going to ask how we were supposed to find out, but I already knew.

We would have to go inside.

As we came closer to the house, it was obvious that no one had lived there for a long,

long time. It was hard to see, but the lawn was very scraggly and overgrown. A few of the windows were broken out. We stood in the darkness, looking at the dark form of the house.

"Come on," Caleb urged quietly. "We're wasting time."

We slipped through the front door.

In the house it was *really* dark. And creepy.

But who was I to call a house creepy? After all . . . I was a ghost! And if we didn't find a home for Robert, I was going to be a ghost for a long, long time.

Suddenly we heard a noise!

It was a scraping sound, like someone dragging something on wood.

We stopped, listening intently.

There it was again! It was coming from a room at the end of a dark hall.

What could it be? A ghost? A person?

Caleb began drifting down the hall, and I followed. We moved slowly, not sure of what was making the noise.

Scraaaaaaaape . . . .

We stopped. It was coming from behind

a closed door.

Now we did have a problem! If it was a ghost that was making the noise, and we slipped through the door, it would probably see us. Then he might be mad because we were in his house!

Caleb made the first move. He drifted forward, and slipped into the door. In the next instant, he was gone.

Not to be left standing in a dark hall alone, I followed him. I slipped through the door easily enough, and found myself in a small room—alone!

Caleb was gone!

25

I was alone in the room!

"Caleb!" I whispered, as quietly as I could. "Caleb? Where are you?"

Silence. I didn't hear anything but the rhythmic chiming of crickets outside. The window was broken and a large piece of glass had fallen out.

Scraaaaaaaape . . . .

If there was ever a time when I just about jumped out of my skin, this was it! The sudden noise surprised me so much that I let out a scream—before I even knew where the scrape had came from!

But there wasn't anything to worry about. The noise came from a tree branch that had grown too close to the house. The limb had hooked itself around the broken window, and whenever a gentle breeze blew, the branch scraped itself back and forth on the rough edge of the glass.

Whew!

But that still didn't tell me where Caleb was!

"Caleb!" I called out again, only louder this time.

Suddenly he appeared right in front of me! He had slipped right up through the floor! I about jumped out of my blue skin.

"Hey," he said.

"Don't do that!" I demanded. "You scared me!"

"Sorry," he replied. "I just wanted to get a quick look at the basement."

"Did you find anything?"

He shook his head. "Nope. Nothing there. So far, so good. Let's keep looking."

Oh, how I hoped the house was empty! I didn't have my watch on, but I knew it was getting closer and closer to midnight. I knew that if we didn't find a home for Robert soon, it would be too late. I wondered how I would tell Mom and Dad that I was a ghost. I'd probably have to write them a letter and leave it on the counter or something. I wouldn't be able to do a lot of the things, simply because no one would see me!

Being a ghost for the rest of my life would not be very much fun.

We floated down the hall and into the living room. The living room was completely empty except for some old chairs.

Next, we went into the kitchen. Again, there wasn't much there. And from there, we went upstairs.

At the top of the stairs, Caleb touched my arm and signaled for me to stop.

"Uh-oh," he whispered. "Look." I looked to where he was pointing.

At the end of the hall there was a blue glow coming from one of the rooms.

A ghost!

We couldn't see it yet, but there was enough of a glow to plainly see that it was coming from a ghost. My spirits fell. I was hoping that we had found an empty house — and a new home for Robert.

"What now?" I asked Caleb.

"Well, we—"

Suddenly his voice was cut short by someone else's voice!

"WHO'S HERE!" a gruff voice bellowed. The ghost came storming out of the room! He was coming right at us!

26

He was the biggest ghost I have ever seen! Not that I've seen a lot of ghosts before, but this ghost was *huge!* He was probably twice the size of Robert!

"Who are you!?!?!?" he demanded. The ghost had a beard and a mustache, and big, muscular arms. He looked like he could snap us both in half! I think even Caleb was a bit afraid.

We backed up a few feet, not sure what to do.

Suddenly the ghost was right in front of us, towering overhead.

"Please, sir," Caleb began. "We didn't mean to bother you. We were just looking for a place for our friend to live."

"Well it's not going to be here! Can't you see this place is already haunted?!?!"

"Well, we can see that now, but we didn't know it before. I'm sorry we disturbed you."

"Well, away with you. This home is taken. If you're looking for a place to haunt, why not try the old Martin farm down the street." He motioned with his thumb. "I hear that place is empty."

I knew the farm he was talking about. We passed the Martin farm every day on the way to school. Mr. Martin was an old man who didn't have a nice bone in his body. I'd heard that he didn't like children and he kept to himself most of the time. In fact, Mr. Martin didn't even go to the store for food—he had it delivered so he didn't have to talk to anyone.

Caleb looked at me. "Do you know the farm?" he asked. I nodded.

"We're sorry to bother you," Caleb said, speaking to the giant ghost before us. "We'll be leaving now, if you don't mind."

"Well, be quick about it. I've got better things to do than bother with you pesky ghosts."

Pesky? Who's pesky?

Regardless, we weren't going to sit around and argue. Caleb began to sink through the floor and I followed him. I must admit—if I ever turned back into a 'human' again, I was going to miss not being able to walk through walls and doors and floors!

Back outside, we wasted no time in heading for the Martin farm. While I didn't really care to have a run-in with Mr. Martin, the fact that I was invisible made me more comfortable. He couldn't be mean to us if he didn't see us.

It only took us a few minutes to drift to the farm. Soon, we were in the driveway. There were a few barns and small buildings around. Mr. Martin had chickens and geese and goats and cows. He had a really big farm, but no hired hands. He did all the work himself.

"Let's go inside," Caleb said, and we floated toward the house. Lights were on in a couple of rooms. We slipped easily inside, right through the front door.

Mr. Martin was sitting in a chair by the fireplace, reading a newspaper. He had no hair, except for little gray tufts just above his ears. Dark rimmed glasses drooped low over his nose, and it looked like he might be nodding off to sleep.

"Come on," Caleb said. "Let's look around. We don't have a lot of time left."

But as we started to drift ahead to check out the other rooms in the house, a low, throaty growl caused us to stop.

It was Mr. Martin's German shepherd!

We hadn't seen him before. The dog had been sleeping at Mr. Martin's feet, but now his head was raised. His ears were up and the hackles on his back stood straight up like soldiers.

Could he see us?

His teeth showed and his nostrils flared. He was looking right at us . . . and *growling!*

Suddenly the dog jumped to his feet. Teeth gnashing, he started to walk toward us!

27

Gulp.

The German shepherd was coming toward us slowly, head down, mouth open. He was growling viciously.

The dog meant *business.*

"Dusty!" Mr. Martin scolded. "What's gotten into you?" The dog, distracted for only a moment, turned to look at Mr. Martin. Then he turned his attention back to us, growling and snarling nastier than ever.

"Dusty, what on earth are you doing?" Mr. Martin set his newspaper on his lap and stared at the dog. Then he looked at us. Or in our direction, anyway. I knew that he couldn't see us.

But could the dog? Could the dog see us?

It sure looked like he could! The dog was looking directly at us.

"What do we do?" I whispered.

"Don't worry," Caleb whispered back. *"He can sense us . . . but he can't see us. Often times, animals are very in tune to ghosts. The dog isn't sure what it senses, though, simply because he can't see us."*

"Can't he hear us?" I asked.

"Maybe the dog can, but Mr. Martin can't. That is, of course, unless we wanted him to hear us."

"Then what are we whispering for?" I asked.

"I don't know . . . you started it."

Meanwhile, Dusty the German shepherd was coming closer and closer. Mr. Martin was watching the animal curiously.

"Dusty . . . what's the matter, boy?"

Just then, Caleb leapt forward! He leapt forward and lunged at the dog!

What was he doing?!?!

Whatever it was, it worked! The dog yelped and spun, running back to hide on the other side of Mr. Martin. The man just laughed.

"Oh, you scaredy-cat," he said to the

whimpering dog. Mr. Martin picked up his paper and continued to read. The dog eyed us suspiciously from the safety of the other side of the chair.

"Come on," Caleb said, and together we drifted down the hall.

"Do you think that Robert would like to live here?" I asked.

"I think it's a fine house," said Caleb. "I think he would like it a lot. He'd have a lot of room to move about."

"But what about Mr. Martin?" I asked. "And the dog? Won't they bother Robert?"

"No, not anymore than you bothered him at your home. Ghosts can just tune those things out. But this house, if it's not already haunted, would be a perfect place for him."

We drifted through the house, through walls and floors, searching for signs of any other ghost or ghosts who might be living there. We couldn't find any.

"I think we've found our place," Caleb said, stopping at the bottom of the stairs. "I think this place is going to be perfect."

A clock chimed in the living room, and I

peered around the corner.

Eleven o'clock! We only had an hour! We had to find the others and bring Robert back here in an hour!

"Let's go get them!" I said frantically. "There's not much time left!"

But it wasn't going to be that easy. Because at that very moment, Robert, Catherine, and Adrian were in trouble.

Big trouble.

28

We hurried back home as fast as we could, taking shortcuts across fields and meadows. The moon was high in the sky, casting a murky glow over the trees and houses.

We passed our house, but didn't see any sign of Adrian, Catherine, or Robert, so we kept on looking. I was getting even more worried.

"We have to find them!" I said. "We're running out of time!"

I think even Caleb was beginning to worry, too. "I wonder where they could be," he said.

Suddenly, as we passed an old home, I saw a bluish glow in the distance.

"Over there!" I said, pointing.

We hurried down a long, winding driveway and found Robert and Catherine standing outside an old run-down home.

"We were just coming to get you," Catherine said. She sounded worried.

"Where's Adrian?" I asked.

"He's inside the house," Robert answered. "But there's a problem."

I waited to hear the bad news.

"We were going through the house," Catherine said. "Adrian walked downstairs to go through the basement . . . but because the house is old, the staircase couldn't support him."

"You mean he *fell?!?!?*" I asked.

"No, no, he's fine," Catherine said. "But he's trapped. Part of the staircase gave way, and when it did, a wall upstairs collapsed, blocking his way out."

"He's . . . he's trapped in the basement?" I stammered. Robert and Catherine nodded.

"We tried to push the door open, but it was no use," Robert said. "We were coming to get you two to help. Maybe all of us would be strong enough."

"Let's go," Caleb said.

We slipped through a wall and into the house, down a hallway and through another wall, then down to the basement. Thankfully, Adrian wasn't hurt.

"Sorry about this, sis," he said to me.

"I'm just glad you're okay," I said. "Come on. Let's all try and force this door open."

All five of us started to push. We pushed as hard as we could, straining with all our might.

But it was no use. Even all five of us together weren't strong enough to force the door open.

And it was getting late! I knew that we had less than an hour to take Robert to his new home.

What would we do?

Finally, Caleb came up with a solution. Well, a solution of *sorts*.

"Well, there is something else we can try," he said. "I think it will work, but it will be pretty risky."

"What?" I asked.

Caleb and Catherine looked at one

another, then at Robert. The three ghosts knew what Caleb was talking about.

"What?" I asked again.

"See how easy it is for the four of us to go through walls and doors and things?" he began. I nodded, and Caleb continued. "That's because we're *ghosts*. Even you, Alex. You can go through doors and walls just as easily as we can. If Adrian was a ghost, he could do the same, and he wouldn't be trapped anymore."

Adrian? Turn Adrian into a ghost?

"Would it work?" I asked.

Caleb nodded. "Yes, I'm sure it would. But the problem is that it's getting close to midnight. If we turn Adrian into a ghost, and don't get Robert to the new house in time, that means you'll *both* be ghosts. Forever."

Gulp.

29

I looked at Adrian, and he looked back at me.

"It looks like it's our only chance, Al," he said.

"Okay," I agreed. "But we'd better hurry. What do we need to do?"

"Quick," said Caleb. "Let's all stand in a circle and hold hands."

We did as he asked. The five of us stood in the basement, holding hands. What was supposed to happen? Would Adrian disappear or something?

After a minute had gone by, I grew impatient. "What is supposed to happen?" I asked.

But just as I said those words, something

strange began to take place!

Adrian began to turn blue! At first it was very faint, and it was hard to see. But he was turning blue! He began to turn into a ghost, just like Caleb and Catherine and Robert . . . and *me!*

"It's working!" Adrian said, looking down at himself. "It's really working!"

Soon, Adrian's body was completely blue. He had a misty, glowing cast . . . just like the rest of us!

"Hooray!" I shouted.

"Let's get moving," said Robert. "There's not much time left."

We all rose and slipped straight up through the floor. Adrian seemed delighted with his new-found talent!

"This is cool!" he said.

"Yeah, it's cool for now," I said. "But it wouldn't be cool to be a ghost for the rest of our lives."

We drifted back up the driveway and out onto the dirt road, across dark fields and meadows, through a forest and over a stream. Finally, after what seemed like hours, we made it to the Martin farm.

"Beautiful," Robert said, as we stood in the driveway facing the huge house. "This will be perfect!"

"There's not a moment to spare!" Caleb said. "We have to get inside the house now!"

We drifted up to a wall and slipped right on through. Adrian giggled at his new-found talent. He thought it was cool to be invisible and to go through walls. I guess I thought it was kind of cool, too. I would probably miss not being a ghost. But I couldn't imagine being a ghost forever!

We floated down the hall and paused at the living room. Mr. Martin was still there, only he had drifted off to sleep. Dusty, the German shepherd, lay at his feet. When we drifted past, he raised his ears and whimpered a tiny bit.

Then I saw the clock.

Oh no!

It was eleven fifty-nine! We had less than a minute!

"What do we do?!?!" I cried frantically.

"Quick!" Catherine said. "To the basement!"

We floated over to a closed door and

swished right on through without even opening it. It was very dark. We were going down a long stairway, down into the basement.

When we reached the floor, we stopped. Robert clicked on a light and looked around.

"This is great!" he said. "This will do nicely. I can live here in peace."

As soon as he said those words, a very strange thing started to happen. Adrian and I became very blue . . . a very bright, radiant blue. We became so bright that the light was almost blinding.

"What's . . . what's happening?" Adrian said.

"It's working!" answered Caleb excitedly. "You're turning back into a human!"

Suddenly, all of our brightness faded. We weren't blue anymore, and both of our feet were on the ground.

"It worked!" I said. "It worked! We're not ghosts anymore!"

Caleb and Catherine seemed pleased. Even Robert, the one who was partly responsible for this mess, seemed happy. He smiled a big grin, and threw his hands up into the air.

"I'm sorry that I got you into this," he said. "But I'm glad it worked out. Now I have a new home, and Caleb and Catherine can return to their home."

Upstairs, I heard the clock chime twelve.

"Whew," I said. "And just in time, too. That was too close."

All of a sudden the basement door flew open!

"Who's down there!" I gruff voice bellowed out. *"I said . . . WHO'S DOWN THERE! I heard voices! Come out, whoever you are!"*

It was Mr. Martin! Now that Adrian and I weren't ghosts anymore, he could hear our voices!

We were trapped in his home!

30

Now what would we do? Here we were in Mr. Martin's basement, in plain view! If Mr. Martin came downstairs, he would be able to see us!

Boy, would we be in trouble then! There would be no way we could possibly explain how we got there or what we were doing. We didn't mean any harm . . . we were just trying to find Robert a new place to haunt . . . and to change ourselves back into regular kids!

But how would we explain that to Mr. Martin?!?! If we told him the truth, and said that we had been ghosts and that we only needed to find a home for Robert, there's no way he would believe us! He'd call Mom and Dad . . . and we'd be grounded for the rest of our lives!

I didn't know what would be worse . . . being a ghost forever—or being *grounded* forever!

Whatever happened, we were going to get into trouble. *Big* trouble.

"Who's down there?!?!?" he demanded again. From where he was, at the top of the basement steps, he couldn't see us . . . but if he came downstairs, we would be in full view! We had to do something!

Suddenly, Adrian pointed to some crates stacked up near a corner.

That was it! If we could slip behind those crates and duck out of sight, maybe Mr. Martin wouldn't see us! It just might work—but we'd have to hurry.

Adrian tip-toed over to the crates, and I followed him. He squeezed in behind the stacked wooden boxes and crouched into a ball. I did exactly what he did, and together we huddled close, keeping our heads down, trying to remain unseen.

There was nothing Caleb, Catherine, or Robert could do. They stood in plain view to us, but they wouldn't be seen by Mr. Martin.

We heard the heavy thump of footsteps on the stairs. Mr. Martin was coming for us!

"Whoever you are, come out now! I heard voices down here! I tell you . . . *I heard voices!!*" He was angry. But I guess if someone was hiding in my basement, I'd be angry, too.

Adrian and I could do nothing except stay as still and quiet as possible, and hope Mr. Martin didn't see us.

Ker-clunk . . . ker-clunk . . . ker-clunk.

Footsteps came down the stairs. We could hear him coming closer and closer.

Ker-clunk . . . ker-clunk. The footsteps stopped.

"Don't want to come out, eh?" Mr. Martin's booming voice echoed through the basement. "All right . . . have it your way. Dusty! Come down here!"

Oh no!! He was calling in his dog! There's no way we could hide from a German shepherd! We'd be caught for sure! We might even go to jail!

Oh, how did we ever get in this much trouble?

31

Upstairs, I heard the sound of nails scratching on wood.

Dusty was coming.

I could hear his paws racing across the floor upstairs. Then I heard him coming down the steps.

"Good boy," Mr. Martin said. "Come on, fella. Go find where those voices came from."

The dog reached the bottom of the stairs.

This was it. We were sure to be caught.

Gulp.

Dusty started growling.

Double gulp.

The growling was coming closer . . . .

Triple gulp.

I was about to stand up right then and there. I knew we were going to be caught, and I didn't want a mean dog after me. I thought that it just might be best to stand up and have Mr. Martin call the dog off.

But right then, just as I was about to stand up, a strange thing happened.

I could hear Dusty growling—but he was going the *other* way! He wasn't anywhere near where we were!

I turned my head and peeked around the corner.

Hooray!

Caleb, Catherine and Robert stood against the far wall. They were smiling, and didn't seem worried at all! The dog was staring at them, growling, but I knew that he couldn't see the ghosts!

"Dusty!" Mr. Martin said. "What are you growling at? There's nothing there, boy!"

The dog continued to hold his ground, snarling and growling, and every once in a while he let out a vicious bark. I could see Caleb, Catherine and Robert standing against the wall, smiling.

"You silly dog!" Mr. Martin scolded. "You're growling at a wall!! There's nothing there! Come here!"

The dog turned and walked back to where Mr. Martin was standing, every once in a while glancing back to growl at the wall.

"I don't know what's gotten into you," the old man said. The dog whimpered. "Well, I guess I was just hearing things," Mr. Martin said, to no one in particular.

Ker-clunk . . . ker-clunk . . . ker clunck.

Footsteps.

Mr. Martin was going back upstairs! It worked!

When we finally heard Mr. Martin reach the top of the stairs and close the door, Adrian and I slowly came out of hiding.

"That was close — *too* close," I whispered.

"We still have one problem," Catherine said, looking at Adrian and I. "We still have to get you out of here without Mr. Martin seeing you."

"Can't you just turn us back into ghosts?" Adrian asked.

"I'm afraid not," Caleb answered. "That

only works once. If we did it again, you would be a ghost forever. There would be no way to reverse it."

Once again, I wondered who made up these silly ghost rules. They didn't seem to make any sense!

"We'll have to wait till Mr. Martin goes to sleep," Adrian said. "That will be our only chance."

"What about Dusty?" I asked. I was more afraid of the German shepherd than I was of Mr. Martin!

"Well," Caleb began. "The three of us are still invisible. Mr. Martin can't see us. And the dog can *sense* us, but he can't *see* us. We can go around the house and let you know when Mr. Martin is asleep. And we can tell you where the dog is, so you can hopefully slip out without attracting his attention."

"That's a great idea!" I said. "This house is so big, we might be able to get out without Mr. Martin or Dusty even noticing!"

It was our only hope.

Adrian and I waited in the basement while Caleb, Catherine and Robert scoured the house for the easiest way out. It seemed like they were gone a long time. We began to wonder if they had gotten into trouble.

Finally, they came back. All three ghosts looked very grim.

"Bad news," Caleb said, shaking his head. "Mr. Martin has fallen asleep in his living room chair. Dusty is right next to him. Wherever we go in the house, we'll have to pass by him—and Dusty, too."

That was *not* good news.

"Whatever we do," Adrian said, "we'd better get started. It's getting late. Mom and Dad have dinner guests, but they'll be leaving soon, if they haven't already. When they go upstairs and find out that we're not in our beds, they're going to flip."

Adrian was right. Whatever we were going to do, we would have to do it now. We couldn't wait a moment longer. We would have to take our chances and try and sneak right past Mr. Martin.

And Dusty.

Reluctantly, Adrian and I tip-toed up the steps.

It was now or never.

32

Thankfully, the stairs weren't squeaky, and by tip-toeing, we made it up to the top without creating any noise. Caleb, Catherine, and Robert went first, slipping through the closed door. Catherine returned through the door in the next instant.

"It's all clear right in front of the door," she said. "He can't see you from here. Neither can Dusty. Go ahead and open the door . . . but be very quiet!"

That was *good* advice.

Adrian reached out and slowly turned the knob. The door opened gently, slowly, and we stepped up and out of the stairwell. Robert was there, and so was Catherine . . . but Caleb was gone.

"Where is Caleb?" I whispered as quietly as I could.

"He had an idea," said Catherine. "He thinks he might be able to distract the dog."

Sure enough, Caleb drifted back down the hall toward us . . . carrying a dog biscuit!

"Mr. Martin has a whole box of these above his stove," he said, smiling. "Maybe I can get the dog to follow me to the other side of the house. That'll give you two time to get out the front door."

That just might work!

"You two stay right here. I'll go see if I can get the dog interested in this biscuit." Caleb was off again, floating down the hall, toward the living room. He stopped, peered in at the sleeping Mr. Martin, and then turned the corner.

Would it work?

He was gone only a minute or so when we saw him backing out of the living room. He was leaning over, holding out the biscuit . . . followed by the German shepherd! I'll bet the dog thought that it was very strange to see a 'floating' biscuit . . . after all, if he couldn't see

Caleb, it would appear to the dog that the biscuit was just floating in mid-air!

But now the test came. Adrian and I were hunkered down in the shadows at the end of the hall, but we were in plain view. If the dog took his eyes off the biscuit, he would see us.

Would it work?

We were about to find out!

33

Caleb, followed by the dog, passed right by us.

Suddenly, Dusty stopped. He stopped almost directly in front of us, but he was still looking at the biscuit.

I couldn't breathe. I couldn't move. I could hear my heart pounding like a bass drum, and I hoped that Dusty didn't hear it, too.

Seconds passed.

Caleb reached out closer to the dog and waved the biscuit right in front of his nose.

The dog lurched forward and grabbed it! It was a tug of war between Caleb and the German shepherd! Caleb held fast to the biscuit with one hand, but the dog had a firm grip of the treat in his teeth!

Suddenly, the dog lost its hold. Caleb had the biscuit in his hand, and he tossed it far down the hall. The biscuit bounced on the carpet, hit the wall, and tumbled to a stop. As soon as it did, Dusty sprang! He raced down the hall and snatched up the biscuit.

Now was our chance!

Dusty was facing the other way, chomping on his biscuit. We could hear him crunching and chewing loudly. Adrian and I crept to our feet and slid down the hall.

"Hurry!" Catherine said. "Dusty is almost finished with his biscuit!"

Yikes!

We passed the living room. Mr. Martin was still asleep, his head angled sideways, his newspaper still open in his lap. He was snoring like a chainsaw.

"Keep going!" Robert said, and we tip-toed as fast as we could around another corner and to the front door.

Almost there. But we'd still have to get outside.

I reached for the door. Thankfully, the knob turned easily. The door squeaked a tiny bit, but not loud enough for the dog or Mr. Martin to notice.

We were just about to leave when Robert stopped us.

"You won't be seeing me again," he said. "I'm sorry for getting you into all this trouble. I hope everything works out okay."

I felt sorry for him. Actually, it wasn't all of his fault, and I told him so.

"Don't worry," I said. "We'll be fine. I hope you like your new home."

"Oh, this is perfect," he said, smiling. "This house is just perfect. Good-bye."

And with that, he just sunk into the floor! Robert was gone.

Suddenly Caleb came around the corner.

"Go!" he said. "The dog is coming! He's going to see you if you don't go right now!"

Adrian and I slipped out the door, followed by Caleb and Catherine.

But Dusty had caught a glimpse of us! He started barking and growling as he ran to the door!

"Run!" Caleb shouted. "Run as fast as you can!"

So we did. I ran, churning my legs as fast as I could. When I looked back, I saw Mr. Martin at the front door. Dusty's barking had awakened him, and he was peering out into the darkness. The porch light was on, and he had a hold of Dusty by the collar.

"Who's out there!?!?!" he yelled. "Who's there!?!?"

"Nobody here except us ghosts!" Caleb shouted back, laughing. But of course, Mr. Martin wouldn't hear him — Caleb was a ghost! I almost burst out laughing myself.

We ran and ran. The night was dark, but we could see okay from the glow of the moon. I was feeling better already. We ran and ran down the dirt road, and didn't stop until we reached our house. There were still a few cars in our driveway, but it looked like most of Mom and Dad's guests were starting to leave.

And so now we had another problem. How were we going to get into the house and to our bedrooms — without being seen?

We hadn't thought about that.

This was going to be tricky.

34

We crept up along side of a parked car and tried to look in the house. I could see adults standing around, talking and laughing. There were only six or seven of them, including Mom and Dad.

How were we going to do this? We would be seen for sure. There was no way we would be able to sneak past anyone in our house.

Suddenly the front door opened. The last of the guests were leaving! Mom and Dad were waving good-bye in the glow of the porch light.

"Come on," Adrian whispered. We had been leaning on the other side of a car . . . one of the guests' cars . . . so we sure couldn't stay there! We'd be seen for sure.

We ran back behind the shed, followed by Caleb and Catherine. It still seemed weird that we could see them, but no one else could.

"Alex, we have to hurry," Adrian said. "Mom and Dad are going to go upstairs to check on us. If we're not in bed . . . ." He didn't finish his sentence. He didn't need to. I knew what would happen.

We had to find a way to get to our bedrooms.

"I've got it!" Adrian suddenly whispered. "There's a ladder in the barn! We can go get it and climb in through your bedroom window!"

He was right! I always keep my bedroom window open, so we would be able to slip right in.

Question was—could we do it in time?

The last car was just leaving, and Mom and Dad gave one final wave, and closed the front door.

There was no time to lose.

We bolted to the barn. It was dark in the barn—like being in a bottle of ink.

"I think the ladder is over here," I heard Adrian whisper in the darkness. Caleb,

Catherine and I followed the sound of his voice.

"Run your hands along the wall," Adrian said. "Dad has it hanging here somewhere, I'm sure of it!"

But in the darkness, it seemed impossible to find anything.

"Hold it!" Catherine said. "I think I found it! I think it's right here!"

I could hear Adrian shuffle toward Catherine in the darkness.

"Good going! This is it, all right. Help me lift it!"

The four of us picked up the ladder and walked as fast as we could to the house. The side where my bedroom was on was dark, so at least we had a little bit of cover.

"Come on," I urged. "We've got to get this thing up against the house!"

We struggled for a moment, but we finally got the ladder leaned up against my window on the second floor.

"Come on!" I whispered to Catherine, but she just shook her head.

"Aren't you coming?" Adrian asked.

"I'm afraid not," Caleb said. "It's late for

us, too."

"But ... where are you going?" I asked. "I thought this was your home?"

"It is," said Catherine. "And it always will be. We'll always be here, but I'm afraid you won't see us again."

"Why ... why not?" I stammered. Caleb and Catherine had become good friends — even if they were ghosts.

"I guess it's those dumb ghost rules that you don't like," Caleb said to me. "Like Catherine said, we'll always be here. It's just that you won't see us. But we'll look in on you from time to time."

Suddenly, the blue glow that had been so bright began to dim. They were fading away!

"Thank you," Catherine was saying. "Thank you for helping us get our home back."

"Wait!" I cried. "Don't go! Not yet!"

But it was too late. They were gone. We were alone in the yard, standing by the ladder.

"Come on Al," Adrian said. "Mom and Dad are going to be upstairs any second." He motioned toward the ladder. "You go first."

I grabbed a rung and began climbing up.

When I reached the window, I climbed in my bedroom and turned around. Adrian was making his way up the ladder. In just a few seconds, he was at the window, climbing into my bedroom.

"Oh no!" he whispered. "What do we do about the ladder?!?!"

We hadn't thought of that.

Adrian suddenly grabbed the top of the ladder and pushed it! He pushed it away from the house, and it fell to the yard below. There was a dull thud as it hit the grass, but at least it wasn't as loud as I thought it would be.

"There," Adrian whispered. "At least Mom and Dad won't see it in your bedroom window. I'll set my alarm and get up early in the morning and drag it back to the barn."

I was about to say something when the light over the stairs clicked on.

Mom and Dad were coming!

35

As quickly and quietly as he could, Adrian tip-toed out of my room, down the hall and to his bedroom. I could hear Mom and Dad talking as they came up the steps.

This was going to be close!

I didn't have time to change into my pajamas, so I just pulled back the covers on the bed and jumped in. I pulled the sheets up to my chin and lay on my side—just as Mom poked her head in the doorway. As she did, I slowly raised my head, pretending that I had just woke up.

"Hi sweetheart," she said. "Sorry to wake you. Did you have fun today?"

"Mmm-hmm," I said, trying to sound

sleepy.

"That's good," she said. "You and Adrian sure were quiet tonight. I guess with everyone here, and everything going on, I didn't see you come back from Stacey's house."

"No, I guess not," I said sleepily.

"Well, sweet dreams. I'll see you in the morning. Oh — and don't forget — we're going to Alpena tomorrow to visit the Blackburns."

"Okay, Mom," I said. The Blackburns were friends that moved away a few years ago. Mark Blackburn was one year older than Adrian and I, and he had an older sister that was seventeen or something. They were both really nice. They moved to Alpena, which is all the way on the other side of the state . . . so we didn't get much of a chance to see them anymore. It would be fun to see them again.

I heard my bedroom door close and Mom walking away.

Whew! I had just barely pulled that one off!

Soon I heard Mom and Dad walking back down the stairs. The light clicked off, and the house became very quiet. The only thing I could hear were the thousands of crickets singing from the field below. Soon I was fast asleep.

In the morning, I awoke to bright sunshine streaming through my window. The crickets were silent, and their steady chiming had been replaced by the sound of chirping birds. It was beautiful.

I got up, surprised to find that I still had my jeans on.

Oh yeah, I remembered. I hadn't had time last night to change before going to bed.

Suddenly I remembered the ladder!

I rushed to the window and looked outside.

It was gone!

I breathed a sigh of relief. Adrian hadn't forgot.

I was going to miss Caleb and Catherine. It was so strange—just yesterday morning, if you would have asked me if I believed in ghosts, I would have said 'no way' . . . but today, I considered two ghosts among my very best friends. Even though I knew that they would always be here in the house, I wouldn't be able to see them.

I was going to miss them a lot. I wondered if I talked to them out loud once in a while if they might hear me.

"Thanks guys," I whispered, just in case.

After I took a shower, I went downstairs. Mom and Dad were still sleeping, so I thought I'd make some toast and cereal.

Boy — did I get a surprise when I went into the kitchen!

36

On the counter . . . in plain site . . . was a glass of ice water! It looked as if it had just been poured!

I was sure that Adrian had gone back to bed after he had put the ladder away, and I knew Mom and Dad were still sleeping!

There was only one way that glass of water had gotten there.

Caleb and Catherine.

I smiled. I think I was actually going to enjoy living in a 'haunted' house!

I made two slices of toast and was finishing up a bowl of corn flakes when Adrian came down the stairs.

"Man," he said quietly, sitting down at the kitchen table. "I just barely made it to bed last night before Dad came to my room. I almost got caught."

"Same here," I said. "Hey . . . guess what?"

"What?" Adrian asked, eyeing my corn flakes. I think he was trying to decide if he wanted corn flakes or a bagel for breakfast.

"Guess what was waiting for me on the counter this morning when I got up?" I asked, smiling.

A smile came to his lips. He knew.

"A glass of water," he said knowingly.

I nodded. "You got it."

He decided on the corn flakes and got up to pour himself a bowl.

"Are Mom and Dad still asleep?" he asked.

"Yeah," I said, in between crunching on my cereal. "It's a good thing that you got up this morning and put the ladder away."

Adrian froze.

"The ladder!" he whispered frantically. *"I forgot to go get it!"* He put down the box of cereal, and was about to dash off.

"Wait a minute!" I said. "You mean to tell

me that you didn't put the ladder away?"

"No! I must've slept through my alarm! Come on! Help me haul it back to the barn!"

"Adrian . . . when I got up this morning, the ladder was gone! It wasn't on the lawn! I thought you got up and moved it."

"*Gone?!?!* How could that be?! I mean—I overslept! I didn't put the ladder away! How did the ladder get moved?!?!?!"

"I don't know, but it's not there now," I said.

"Do you think Dad or Mom found it?" Adrian asked, his eyes growing wide.

"Nope," I said, smiling. "I'll bet Caleb and Catherine found it. I'll bet they found it and put it away for us."

Sure enough, when we went to look for the ladder, it was right where it belonged—hanging long ways in the barn.

"Cool!" Adrian said as we left the barn. "Caleb and Catherine . . . if you can hear us . . . thank you! Thanks a lot!"

We laughed.

When we returned to the kitchen, we both stopped.

There, on the counter, were two glasses of ice water.

37

Later that morning, we left for Alpena. The ride was long. I read a book, and Adrian listened to his portable CD player. They were my CD's of course. Adrian never has enough money for CD's because he spends it all on comic books.

Finally, we arrived at the Blackburns. I saw Mark's older sister Deana washing her car in the driveway. She smiled and waved when we pulled up. She gave Mom and Dad a hug, then me, then Adrian. Adrian likes Deana, but he'll never admit it. Deana is very pretty.

"Where's Mark?" Adrian asked.

"I don't know," Deana said. "He's been gone all day. I know he went down to the park with some friends, but I haven't seen him."

We went in the house and said 'hi' to Mr. and Mrs. Blackburn, then decided to go look for Mark.

"I'm sure he's down by the park somewhere," Mrs. Blackburn said. "When you find him, make sure that you don't stay out too long. We're having a barbeque, and the food will be ready soon. You kids can go back out later this afternoon, anyway."

We promised that we'd find Mark and that we wouldn't stay long.

The walk to the park wasn't far. The Blackburns live right near the center of town, so we walked down Chisolm street all the way down to Lake Huron. That's another Great Lake. In Petoskey, we have Lake Michigan. In Alpena, they have Lake Huron.

We walked along by the docks for a few minutes. It was a beautiful day. There were lots of boats on the water, and even a few windsurfers and jet skiers. I wished that I had remembered to bring my swim suit!

When we walked over by the park, I heard someone shout our names.

"Adrian!! Alex!!"

It was Mark!

He came running across the grass toward us. He looked the same as the last time we had seen him . . . same blonde hair, same everything. Mark was cool. I couldn't wait to tell him about Caleb and Catherine! He wasn't going to believe that we live in a *real* haunted house!

"Hey, man!" Adrian said, high-fiving Mark as he approached. He looked at me.

"Hey, Alex," he said. He was out of breath.

"Hi Mark," I answered.

"Man, am I glad to see you guys again!" Mark said. His voice was filled with excitement. "You two are probably the only ones who'll believe me!"

Huh?

"What do you mean?" Adrian asked.

"You guys aren't going to believe this — but there were space aliens — *real* space aliens — right here in Alpena!"

"You've *got* to be kidding," I said. I didn't believe in space aliens.

But then again, up until yesterday, I hadn't believed in poltergeists, either!

"This I've got to hear," Adrian said.

"Let's go sit down," Mark said. "This is going to blow you away!"

Next in the 'Michigan Chillers' series . . . .
#4 — 'Aliens Attack Alpena!'
Go to the next page for a few sample chapters!

Boring.

That's how you can describe my life. B-O-R-I-N-G. Nothing exciting ever happens to me. *Nothing.* Well, once I found a twenty-dollar bill while swimming in Hubbard Lake. That was exciting, I guess. But on the level, I think I lead the most boring life in the world.

Little did I know that was all about to change.

It was Monday morning. Another *boring* Monday morning, I might add. First, I have to ride the school bus. Today, of all people, Greg Daniels sat behind me when he got on the bus. He's a wrestler. Which, I guess, isn't so bad, but Greg likes to pick on people.

Especially *me.*

All the kids on the bus were talking about

the meteor that was sighted in the sky over Alpena last night. I didn't see it, but Dad said that he did. He said that it was a bright ball of fire that swooped overhead. He said it looked like it landed in Lake Huron. That's one of Michigan's Great Lakes. Alpena is a city right next to it. That's where I live.

I was talking to my friend Zack about the meteor. Zack is my age and we have a few classes together.

"Man, that meteor was really cool!" he said.

"Did you see it?" I asked.

"Yeah!" Zack answered, bobbing his head. "It was awesome! It was a big streak that soared across the sky." As he spoke, he swung his arm from left to right, imitating a streaking, falling star.

See? I miss all the good stuff.

Boring. That's my life.

Suddenly, I felt a hard smack against the side of my head. It hurt! I didn't have to look—I already knew who it was.

Greg Daniels.

He had whacked me up side the head

with the palm of his hand. He does that just to annoy people. He likes annoying people . . . and messing up their hair.

"Cut it out!" I said, turning my head as I spoke.

"Oh, and what are *you* going to do about it, twerp?" he sneered, his dark eyes glaring at me. His hand snapped up and he smacked me again, this time even harder. "Come on," he challenged. "Wanna fight?"

See what I mean? He's nothing but a troublemaker.

"No," I answered sharply, turning back around to face the front of the bus. But I knew it wasn't over.

"I know you won't fight me, because you're a chicken. Bock, bock-bock, bock, bock," he cackled. He sounded just like a chicken! "You're just chicken and you know it, Blackburn," he finished.

That's my last name. Blackburn. Mark Blackburn. But Greg hardly ever calls anyone by their first name. He usually uses their last name. Not only is he a bully . . . but he's a *rude* bully. Greg is thirteen. I'm twelve, but I'll be thirteen in two weeks. Hooray! A teenager. I can't wait.

Of course, if I get into a fight with Greg Daniels, I might not *live* to see my thirteenth birthday! Greg is a lot bigger . . . and stronger than I am.

I did *not* want to get into a fight with Greg Daniels.

But, as luck would have it, it looked like a fight was going to be unavoidable. Here's what happened:

Greg always gets off the bus first. He usually jumps up out of his seat and pushes other kids out of his way so he can be the first off the bus.

When we got to school, Greg jumped up even before the bus had stopped.

"See ya later, chicken," he said to me as he stood up. As soon as he stepped out into the aisle and started forward, he stumbled . . . and fell flat on his face!

Everyone on the bus laughed at him. Even me! It *was* pretty funny. I think he got what he deserved.

But it looked like I was about to get what

I *didn't* deserve!

Greg had tripped over my backpack! He didn't see it on the floor, and he tripped, falling forward and landing smack dab in the middle of the aisle.

The other kids on the bus were still laughing as he stood up and turned around. He looked down and saw my olive-green backpack, then glared at me.

He was *mad!* His dark eyebrows were scrunched together, and his forehead was wrinkled. His hair was messed up and his face was as red as a tomato.

"You're going to pay for this one, chicken," he said bitingly, clenching his teeth together.

He stepped closer, leaning toward me. "Get ready to get creamed, chicken. Your luck has just run out."

I closed my eyes, waiting for the worst.

2

"Greg, knock it off," the bus driver suddenly boomed. Greg turned away and saw the bus driver looking at him, then turned back to me.

"You're going to pay for this, chicken," he said in a quieter voice that still trembled with fury. *"Wait till I see you on the bus tonight. You'll pay for this."*

Great. I might as well just make out my will right now. I'm going to die. Looks like I won't live to see my thirteenth birthday, after all.

Well, at least my short life wasn't so boring anymore.

All day long, I did nothing but worry about the bus trip home. I couldn't even pay attention in class. In my history class, we had a movie about the American revolution. Then we had a quiz afterwards, and I missed almost every question.

In my English class, I sit next to Carly Andrews. I have to admit, I really have a crush on her. She has long, blonde hair and she's very pretty.

But I was so wigged-out about the bus ride home, I couldn't even *think* about her!

In science class, all we did was talk about the meteor. My teacher explained that meteors are pieces of space rock that fly through space very fast. Once in a while, they enter the earth's atmosphere. Most of them burn up before they hit the earth's surface, but a few of them don't.

Like the one last night. On the news, they said the meteor had crashed into Lake Huron. I was really interested, but I was too worried about getting decked by Greg Daniels.

Then, in my last class, I had an idea. Actually, the idea was given to me by my friend, Meghan. I've known her ever since the first grade. She's one of my best friends. Meghan has short brown hair and she's the exact same height as I am.

She leaned over to talk to me when the teacher wasn't looking.

"I heard you're going to fight Greg Daniels on the bus," she whispered.

Great. I think the whole school knew I was going to get creamed. Maybe somebody should sell tickets.

"Well, I sure don't want to," I whispered back.

"What did you do to make him so mad at you?" she asked. Her eyes were wide. I'm sure she knew that there was no way I could win a fight with Greg Daniels.

When I told her how Greg had tripped over my backpack, she started laughing. "Good!" she hissed. "It's about time he gets a taste of his own medicine."

"The problem is, that medicine is going to be hard for me to swallow on the bus ride home," I said quietly, shaking my head.

We were both silent for a few moments. Meghan went back to writing something, then she stopped. She turned her head toward me, her eyes all big and round.

"Hey, I've got an idea!" she whispered. "Why don't you just 'miss' the bus? I mean . . . you don't have to ride the bus home."

"I thought about that," I said. And I had. I thought that if I didn't ride the bus home, then I wouldn't have to fight Greg. But how would I get home? I lived ten miles from school. I certainly couldn't walk ten miles!

"You could ride my brother's mountain bike home," Meghan offered. "He won't care. We only live a couple blocks from the school. We can walk there. You can take his bike."

Now *that* was an idea. Ten miles is a long way to go, but if I had a bicycle . . . .

"You really think that he wouldn't mind if I borrowed his bike?" I whispered, trying to keep silent so that our teacher wouldn't hear.

"Nah. He's pretty cool. I'm sure it would be okay with him."

Suddenly, my spirits were lifted. Maybe I might live to see my thirteenth birthday, after all.

"Meet me behind the school and we'll walk to my house," Meghan said.

When class was over I had to walk through the hall to my locker. Man, I hoped I didn't run into Greg! He might decide that he wasn't going to wait till I got on the bus.

Thankfully, I didn't see him.

That is, of course, until I went outside . . .

3

He was waiting for me.

Right outside the doors of the school.

"Ready to die, chicken?" he sneered. His hands were doubled into fists, ready for action. A group of other kids started to gather around.

This was it. I was a goner.

Greg took a step forward, and I took a step back.

"What's the matter, chicken?" he mocked. "Bock, bock, bock-bock, bock . . . ."

Soon all of the other kids around were doing the same thing.

"Bock, bock-bock, bock, bock-bock," the group chanted.

I took another step back and bumped into someone. The chanting suddenly stopped, and I spun.

It was the principal, Mr. Greene. Mr. Greene is short and hardly has any hair. He's a nice guy, and most kids like him.

Was I ever glad to see *him!*

"I think that will be just about enough of this horseplay," he said, speaking to the small crowd that had gathered. "Go on. You all have buses to catch."

Saved! Well . . . at least for the time being.

The crowd of kids began to thin out, and I caught a glimpse of Meghan. She was standing by the sidewalk at the end of a line of buses. She nodded her head, indicating for me to sneak away.

Greg Daniels turned and began walking toward the bus. He glanced over his shoulder every few seconds to make sure I was coming.

I had an idea. If I could make Greg just *think* that I was coming, then he would get on the bus! When he did, I could take off running! There's no way he would be able to do anything!

It was the only chance I had.

I slowly began walking toward the bus. There was a short line of students waiting to get on. Greg was in the back, so I walked slow.

Come on, I thought. *Hurry up and get on the bus. Hurry up . . . .*

It seemed to take forever for him to board the bus. I watched him take a step up, then another, then look back over his shoulder at me. He had this really sick grin on his face. I think he would really enjoy beating me up.

Finally, I was the last one standing at the door of the bus.

"Well?" the bus driver asked. "Are you riding, or aren't you?"

Now was my chance!

I turned and ran as fast as I could. My sneakers smacked on the pavement as I bolted along the row of parked buses. I carried my backpack in one hand, swinging it madly back and forth as I sprinted down the sidewalk.

I saw Meghan up ahead of me. She had been waiting, wondering what I was going to do.

I managed a quick glance behind me, and what I saw sent a wave of terror through my body.

Greg.

He had gotten off the bus somehow, and

now he was in hot pursuit! I could hear his footsteps thundering behind me.

This was a nightmare! I didn't think Greg would be able to get off the bus. I thought that once he was on the bus, he'd be stuck.

Could I outrun him?

I had to. I just *had* to.

So much for my boring life!

Fear can make you do funny things, sometimes. Just seeing Greg made me run even faster. I was determined that I would outrun him.

I caught up to Meghan and she started running with me.

"This way!" she yelled, pointing toward the forest. "I know a trail! If we can get there, we can lose him in the forest!"

I hoped she was right.

Behind us, Greg seemed to be getting tired. He wasn't running as fast, and we had been able to put some distance between us.

But he was still chasing us, fast and furious.

"I'm going to get you, chicken!" he shouted. *"You're in for it now!"* He was as mad as ever.

"Over there!" Meghan heaved, as we jumped over branches and brush. I hoped she knew where she was going!

The woods became thicker and thicker. Branches tore at my arms and face, and we couldn't run very fast. Once I almost tripped and fell.

Suddenly, we came to a trail! Meghan was right!

But we could still hear Greg behind us, trudging through the thick forest.

"You just wait, chicken!" he shouted.

"Come on!" Meghan yelled frantically as she started up the path. "We can hide in the woods!"

"Where does this path go?" I managed to ask between heavy gulps of air. I was getting tired of running. The forest was dense and the branches were thick.

"It goes way back into the forest," she answered. "But there's lots of places to hide. Over here!"

Suddenly, she bolted off of the trail and went behind a thick clump of small willows. I couldn't see her!

"Where are you?" I asked.

"Shhhh!" she replied in a voice just above a whisper. *"I'm right here!"*

I took a few steps toward the willows and sure enough, she was crouched down low. It was almost impossible to see her! The branches were very thick.

I fell to the ground and rolled sideways next to Meghan. The only thing I could hear was the sound of my own heart beating. And birds. Lots of birds sang from high in the trees.

We waited.

"Do you think we've lost him?" I whispered between heaving breaths.

"I don't know," Meghan answered.

In an instant, we knew. We could hear the crunching of footsteps along the trail, not far away.

Had he seen us? Did he know we had left the trail?

Suddenly, we heard Greg's voice.

"I know you're out here somewhere," he said, his voice raised in anger.

I shuddered. If he found me now, I would *really* get it!

"Uh-oh," I heard Greg say in a mocking voice. "Hey, chicken . . . *I can seeeee yooouuuu.*"

Suddenly, I heard breaking branches and the crunching of footsteps.

Greg had found us! He had found our hiding place!

4

All of a sudden, Meghan burst up from the ground and began running . . . *deeper into the swamp!*

I had no choice. I jumped up and ran after her.

Behind us, I could hear Greg lumbering through the branches. Twigs snapped and popped as he took up chase. It was harder going for Greg, since he was so much bigger than Meghan and I.

The forest grew thicker, but Meghan pressed on, pushing limbs out of her way as we trudged through the dense underbrush. We kept going for what seemed like hours.

Finally, Meghan stopped and turned to look behind us. I did the same.

There was no sign of Greg. We stood for a few minutes, listening for any sign of him plowing through the woods, but there was none. The forest was quiet, except for the peaceful chirping of birds.

"Whew," I said, breathing a sigh of relief. "That was close."

Meghan opened her mouth to speak, but she was interrupted by a strange noise in the distance. It sounded like a radio being tuned.

"What on earth is that?" she said.

We listened. The noise became a low hum. But we couldn't see where it was coming from.

"I think it's coming from over there, on the other side of those cedar trees," I said, pointing with my arm.

Meghan turned and led the way, and I followed. The humming grew louder.

We crept up to a line of cedars and crouched down. Whatever was making the noise was just on the other side of the trees.

I thought that it might be a small factory of some sort . . . but I've never heard of a factory in the middle of the woods!

Slowly, very slowly, I crept up and peeked through the branches.

"Whoaaa!!" I whispered. I froze. My eyes grew wide and my jaw fell.

"What is it?" Meghan asked, getting to her feet.

There was no way I could explain it. This she would have to see for herself.

Sitting in a small clearing was a spaceship! There was no doubt about it. It was egg-shaped and silver, about the size of a large van. Two antennas protruded out of the top. There were no windows, but there was a door on the side, and a row of blue and green flashing lights that went all around the middle. The lights flashed and chased around the ship like a string of Christmas lights.

Meghan's mouth opened, but no sound came out. Neither of us spoke.

"It's . . . it's a spaceship," she finally whispered.

I had only *heard* stories about spaceships before. I read somewhere about some spaceship that was supposed to have crashed about fifty years ago, and someone was keeping the remains of the spaceship in their locked garage. I didn't know if it was true or not.

All of a sudden the humming stopped. The flashing lights blinked a few more times and then went out. All was quiet.

Except—

A door was opening! The door of the spaceship began to screech open! Someone—or *something*—was coming out!

About the author

Johnathan Rand is the author of the best-selling **'Chillers'** series, now with over 1,000,000 copies in print. In addition to the **'Chillers'** series, Rand is also the author of **'Ghost in the Graveyard'**, a collection of thrilling, original short stories featuring *The Adventure Club*. (And don't forget to check out **www.ghostinthegraveyard.com** and read an **entire story** from 'Ghost in the Graveyard' ***FREE!***) When Mr. Rand and his wife are not traveling to schools and book signings, they live in a small town in northern lower Michigan with their two dogs, Abby and Salty. He still writes all of his books in the wee hours of the morning, and still submits all manuscripts by mail. He is currently working on his newest series, entitled **'American Chillers'**. His popular website features hundreds of photographs, stories, and art work. Visit:

www.americanchillers.com

For information on personal appearances, motivational speaking engagements, or book signings, write to:

AudioCraft Publishing, Inc.
PO Box 281
Topinabee Island, MI 49791

or call
(231) 238-0297

About the cover art: This unique cover was designed and created by Michigan artists Darrin Brege and Mark Thompson.

Darrin Brege works as an animator by day, and is now applying his talents on the internet, creating various web sites and flash animations. He attended animation school in southern California in the early nineties, and over the years has created original characters and animations for Warner Bros (Space Jam), for Hasbro (Tonka Joe Multimedia line), Universal Pictures (Bullwinkle and Fractured Fairy Tales CD Roms), and Disney. Besides art, he and his wife Karen are improv performers featured weekly at Mark Ridley's Comedy Castle over the last eight years. Improvisational comedy has provided the groundwork for a successful voice over career as well. Darrin has dozens of characters and impersonations in his portfolio. Darrin and Karen have a son named Mick.

Mark Thompson has been a professional illustrator for 25 years. He has applied his talents with toy companies Hasbro and Mattel, along with creating art for automobile companies. His work has been seen from San Diego Seaworld to Kmart stores, as well as the Detroit Tigers and the renowned 'Screams' ice-cream parlor in Hell, Michigan. Mark currently is designing holiday crafts for a local company, as well as doing website design and digital art from his home studio. He loves sci-fi and monster art, and also collects comics for a hobby. He has two boys of his own, and they're BIG Chiller Fans!

All AudioCraft books are proudly printed, bound, and manufactured in the United States of America, utilizing American resources, labor, and materials.

USA